Also by David Rabe

Plays

The Black Monk (based on a story by Chekhov)
The Dog Problem
Cosmologies
A Question of Mercy (based on the diary of Richard Selzer)
Those the River Keeps
Hurlyburly
Goose and Tomtom
In the Boom Boom Room

The Vietnam Plays

Streamers
The Orphan
Sticks and Bones
The Basic Training of Pavlo Hummel

Fiction

Dinosaurs on the Roof
A Primitive Heart
Recital of the Dog

Children's Books

Mr. Wellington

GIRL
BY THE
ROAD
AT
NIGHT

A NOVEL OF VIETNAM

DAVID RABE

Simon & Schuster
New York London Toronto Sydney

Simon & Schuster
1230 Avenue of the Americas
New York, NY 10020

First Simon & Schuster hardcover edition June 2010

SIMON & SCHUSTER and colophon are registered trademarks of Simon & Schuster, Inc.

John Balaban, translator, "Love Lament" from *Ca Dao Viet Nam: Vietnamese Folk Poetry*. Translation © 2003 by John Balaban. Reprinted with the permission of Copper Canyon Press, www.coppercanyonpress.org.

For information about special discounts for bulk purchases, please contact Simon & Schuster Special Sales at 1-866-506-1949 or business@simonandschuster.com.

The Simon & Schuster Speakers Bureau can bring authors to your live event. For more information or to book an event contact the Simon & Schuster Speakers Bureau at 1-866-248-3049 or visit our website at www.simonspeakers.com.

Designed by Jill Putorti

Manufactured in the United States of America

10 9 8 7 6 5 4 3 2 1

Library of Congress Cataloging-in-Publication Data
Rabe, David.
    Girl by the road at night: a novel of Vietnam/David Rabe.
        p. cm.
    1. Vietnam War, 1961–1975—Fiction. 2. Vietnam—Fiction. I. Title.
    PS3568.A23G57 2010
    813'.54—dc22
            2009048673

ISBN 978-1-4391-6334-4

For Jill

You wander around on your own little cloud
When you don't see the why, or the wherefore.

"DON'T SLEEP IN THE SUBWAY,"
PETULA CLARK

Stepping into the field: sadness fills my deep heart.
Bundling rice sheaves: tears dart in two streaks.
Who made me miss the ferry leaving?
Who made this shallow creek that parts both sides?

CA DAO,
TRANSLATED BY
JOHN BALABAN

GIRL

BY THE

ROAD

AT

NIGHT

1

Consider, first of all, that Pfc Whitaker awakes in his Fort Meade, Maryland, barracks in the early morning, sweating. He stares through unshifting, dust-speckled air and sees beams of rough-hewn wood. Looking at their splintering surfaces and thinking of the long, barren days ahead, the hours of his final weekend of freedom in which he has nothing to do, he feels sad. He feels like a man who's been ordered to leave the earth, his destination the moon. He must live in Vietnam for a year.

In the latrine he flushes a bug down the toilet and his mood is reflected in the insect's futile flailing. The flood and dark of the drain take it away. He wonders, Does it scream?

Now he paces slowly in the hall and Sharon is only a feeble flickering in some small corner of his brain. He does not really see her perfect legs and hard, creamy little tits. She is unremembered. He sees his moving feet on the floor. He does not see her black hair that lay stuck in sweat to her lips. She spoke of Wall Street, of the stock market, as if she understood what she was saying. He does not remember her hot buttocks burning in his hands. She sucked blood from his throat, coming. Pacing, he crosses his arms. He does not remember. His genitals stir, his prick nearly grows.

He is thinking of going to Washington, D.C. There is to be a peace march, he's heard. A protest against this war. I will protest, he thinks, knowing he lies, though he has a truckload of urges and reasons. He will see the monuments to Lincoln and George Washington. He will see the crowds. He will go to the Washington Monument and look up its long, thin length. He feels the edges and tentacles of other thoughts stirring. He shuts them out. He showers and dresses in wrinkled clothing, yet he places a carefully folded tie in his pocket and he buffs his already shiny shoes.

Crossing to his footlocker, he rummages among papers and socks. There are those on post who say a man is a fool to go to Vietnam. Not many, but some, their voices smug, bitter, secretive. It makes him ache to hear them. In a blind, unspeakable wish for denial, he listens. Is it to hear more today that he is going to travel? Is it to risk hearing, finally, a word, theory, fact, or statistic that will make him believe? Does he hope to believe? Or is it to prove them foolish, to prove by being among them a full day and finding nothing in all their placards, slogans, and cries, that there is in fact nothing there to find?

From his locker, he takes a copy of his orders, which he folds precisely to fit his pocket as he moves toward the door.

Only those men on KP, CQ, or guard are in the company

area—all others having departed on passes at the end of the Friday workday—so he sees no one as he crosses the small space of worn grass between the barracks and the white, shed-like headquarters building. He opens the frayed and patched screen door. Thornberg, the CQ, is tilted and twitching in uneasy sleep at the desk, an open comic book teetering on his limp hands. Whitaker stands a moment, thinking. Then he takes his pass from its slot in the green rectangular pass book before adding his name and time of departure to the long list of other names and times already scribbled onto the blocks of the sign-out sheet. He tiptoes out into the white wind. He puts the card of his pass in his billfold and shoves his billfold deep into his right-hip pocket.

Far up the gray road, past the few trees, a bright green bench stands beneath a faded bus stop sign. He makes a fist with each hand, and thumps his chest. He begins to jog.

2

Consider now that Quach Ngoc Lan is Vietnamese and lives in a place that is a burgeoning jungle; think of incessant heat and dirt pressed into the substance of skin, calluses that go to the bone, seasons possessed by rain followed by seasons of dust. Think of being as small as a thin child, forever. Consider that nothing starts with any single event, and then hear a far-off gunshot and see a small dark girl turn round to squint across paddies of water and rice. She finds no soldiers anywhere in view. There are only laborers, bowing over as if whispering to the water in which they stand. One straightens. Lan listens. She is watching, concernedly. Other figures move along carrying baskets used in irrigation. As always in these months there have been only the lightest showers. She blinks. On the retaining wall someone stands idle near a parked bicycle. Water is being sent from the ditch to the field by a pair of men pulling ropes that lift a large sack, gushing and spilling, as it swings forward to tilt and empty. Perhaps they sing for a helpful rhythm. They are too far off for her to hear, but in her thinking there is such a song, while the wilderness beyond is eerie in the failing light. Rice stalks, why do you smile at me? her father would sing as he worked. Lan's tawny feet are set in the brown dirt of a path that slants through weeds. An opening to a cistern is near, the edges damp. A pinheaded snake slithers past. The snake is a line of quick blue light among the weeds and over the path running between several tin-walled adjoining shanties. Something clatters. She turns. Inside, she knows, there is a bed, a broken whiskey bottle, and a thickish drunken GI trying to dress himself. Does he now tug at his trousers to get them over his sticky, hairy legs? Does he blink, belch, nearly vomit? His brows must shine with sweat.

Lan has put one finger to her mouth. There has been no further firing. Light is soft upon the slanting metal of the shanty rooftops, though it seems to collect strangely at the higher edges. There have been countless soldiers lying on her, pumping and grunting throughout the day; now they float in memory, their multiple bodies assembled as a single phantom hovering somewhere far off. She does not think of them.

She is looking onto the fields where the workers move in the ankle-deep water. Color is subdued, the air grown dull. She has memories of performing such tasks in similar water. At the rim of the forest, the sky holds merely remnants of its earlier powerful heat. The wavering dark will soon become a black cloud wiping away the day.

The GI falls behind her on the path. She hears and looks. He pounds the ground, kneels. His shirt is red with a semi-mandarin collar. A tiger's head, making a slight splash of gold, is embroidered onto the bright blaze of the cloth above the pocket. His neck is brawny, his shoulders thick and knotted. He is broad and short. He wanted her to lick and suck him until he was hard when they were on the bed in the shanty. His wrinkled prick had swollen slowly, swaying; and when she lay back to open herself between her legs, something odd passed across his eyes; he grabbed her head, pressed it down against his hardness, poking her cheek, hitting her nose. She adjusted and did as he wished, cheating and using her fingers as soon as he relaxed a little. The spurts started without warning, and he looked startled, as if she had done something wrong. He grabbed for her and she pulled away, giggling, but wary of him, fearful of his wild, unhappy eyes. He grimaced, held himself, sat there pulsing, rubbing, sweating.

Now he is kneeling and drunk in a patch of weeds. It seems impossible that he, so huge, was ever intensely concerned with such thinness as her—her little bones—though she knows he was. He is struggling, almost risen. He wears dark glasses. And for a moment she feels a kind of tenderness toward him. She feels as if she is touching his eyes, his nostrils, his ears and wide mouth. She is a shadow touching a shadow to no purpose. She has not actually moved, but stands watching him try to stuff his shirttail into his trousers. He seems ignorant of the fact that the task is being made difficult by his already-buckled belt. He is so awkward. Where do they come from? Her shadow hand draws back; he grunts and lets the shirttail go. It falls and flaps. "You same-same Vietnamee," she says to him and titters.

He turns; the black glasses point at her, but he does not speak.

"You do shirt—you same-same. Yeah. Yeah." She is grinning. It seems to her that his untucked shirt hanging over his trousers follows a custom more Vietnamese than American. "Ho Chi Minh, you," she says.

He steps sharply at the sound of the name. "Shut up. Talk shit."

She is beaming, nodding; they always have something to say if they are called that old man's name: Ho Chi Minh.

"I no want you talk me, pig."

"Okay. Hello."

"You stupid, you 'stand?"

"I know."

"You number goddamn fucking ten."

"I don't know."

"I'm tellin' you."

"Hello."

"Fuck-face."

"No sweat, GI."

"'Cause you're jus' shit, you understand me. Yes, you are, no matter what they say. Any of them. None of them." Looking dizzy, he goes hopping sideways. "I want to take you home. Take you home. Because you're all any man could ask for. You understand? Intercourse. Fucking. We'll settle down." She can't tell if he's trying to laugh. "You'd be a smash," he sputters, then coughs, nodding with little downward jerks of his head that are so fast they seem a kind of crazy spasm.

"Toi khong biet," she says. "I no 'stand." They are indecipherable, all of them; their moods shatter, cruel and dangerous as the beer bottles that break. She wishes she had not tried to play and joke with him. She has moved backward from him. He stares at her bitterly. She stands amid palm trees, a thicket

of wrinkled, curving trunks. She wants to look away. They have no sense, no understanding of how to behave. Do they have no shame the way they want to look right at you? She wants to spit at him. She wishes he would vanish from her sight, sink into the earth. Why does he not go? I am Quach Ngoc Lan, she thinks. No more. Do you want dirt? Go. I am no more. I am all dirt. I will beat you. "I will beat you, GI," she says. "I will kill you."

He laughs. He clenches his hands and punches nothing with them, like a fool who thinks he can hurt the air.

"No, no, no, no." If only she could speak so he could understand, she would tell him of the boy she punished two days ago, pounding until water gushed from his eyes, blood stained his mouth. She took a switch and beat his legs. Now she yells, "Oh, babysan! I fini him. Get outta here. You love a babysan, GI? Babysan numba ten. Take many my things I have. You don't know. Same-same babysan. Get outta here. I am very happy. Always very happy. Love GIs. Everybody good. Vietnamee all happy. Everybody good."

"One beer!" he yells. "One beer!" and turns away to bounce off toward the roadside building where the beer is kept. Inside the blue stone walls there are benches, chairs, and tables strewn with comic books, other magazines of guns and shooting, and *Playboys* with shiny pictures of big naked American girls, all gathered for the soldiers who come throughout the burning days. They loll about, while their vehicle, truck or jeep, is hosed and scrubbed clean on the front driveway by yelping, half-clad boys. Drinking Coke or beer, they study and fondle the four or five girls who drift about the room in waves of sun and dust. The soldiers drink and the girls chatter; they touch the soldiers, rub their thighs. The soldiers laugh. The trucks and jeeps arrive and go. The road is full of dust, clouds stirred by the rumbling wheels, dimming the air and falling back upon them in a skin of grime so that the car wash is always busy. Beds are kept in shanties a short distance from the road, and Trojan rubbers and postcards and trinkets are sold along the pathway that winds at a slight decline to the shanties.

Turning, Lan sees the snake move. It squiggles and darts. Peculiar bubbles of light appear in a leaden smear afloat in front of her narrowing eyes. She coughs, tastes sweetness that turns into bile demanding she spit.

3

Unlike Lan, Pfc Joseph Whitaker knows American soldiers are not at all indecipherable, but rather they are simple, witty, tough, straightforward, and strong. Yet he sits, brooding and a little lonely at the counter of a bus terminal cafeteria in Washington, D.C., trying to use the melody and lyrics of a pop tune on a radio he can scarcely hear to arouse some good and hopeful feeling. But all the careful amplification of its production is gone; it comes out crippled from the red plastic cheapness of the transistor radio the waitress keeps stashed under the counter. She snaps her gum. Go on, you big babe, Whitaker thinks. You big babe. Over coffee, he has been considering his future in the war zone and daydreaming the slow disintegration of his body. My Body Exploding, he has called it, A Cartoon. At the periphery of his mind, the waitress floats, while images at the center show his skin, muscle, and bone coming apart before his eyes. It is a graceful sequence, like one of those grade school educational films in which a flower bursts from a seed to bloom, only in Whitaker's version, the flower, Whitaker, goes from blooming to debris. He sits with his chin in his hands.

Looking at the neat double curves of the waitress's buttocks packaged in her crisp uniform, he grins, thinking of his wounds: I'll suck your tits, kiss your sweet snatch. "May I have a little more coffee, Nurse?" he says.

"I'm sorry."

He wants to ask her if she did something wrong, but instead he says, "What?"

"I didn't hear you."

"More coffee," he says.

"No, I mean what you called me."

"Nurse?"

"Yeah?"

"What do you think about me having to go to Vietnam?"

"Didn't know you were."

"It's what's happenin'."

"Too bad."

"Is that all?"

"Hazardous to your health, hon." She smiles at him, and her cheeks wrinkle with the movement of the muscles. Her hair is stiff. He notices the layered, leftover lacquer of old hair spray, the powder thick on her face.

"It's your bedside manner," he says as she shrugs and wanders off. He watches, feeling insulted, because obviously she has decided he is a nuisance. It's disillusioning. Who would have thought a nurse could stoop so low? And he, a wounded crippled lonely soldier boy.

He frowns at the cup of coffee she has left before him. He resents being alone. On the grounds of the Washington Monument, the Lincoln Memorial, what is occurring? Are they marching? Smoking pot, talking, balling, nothing? He doesn't know, and he'll never know if he stays in this stupid bus station, when it was for the purpose of maybe seeing what was happening that he came to town in the first place? All dressed up in shabby civilian clothing but bearing in his pocket a neatly folded copy of his orders to go to the war—his name listed and circled. To what purpose? To show people? He knows better than to think that the people at the march, made aware of the decree in his pocket, would look at him with wonder, with pity, with respect or tenderness. Their rejection feels biting and directed at him personally, and he hates them for it. Should they notice him at all, it would be, he is sure, in the way the blessedly healthy look at cripples. Fingering the shape of the papers outlining his fate beneath the cloth of his jacket, he is bewildered by the power of the document. He stares, wondering at the lengths of time and blue ocean between this cafeteria and that far-off land. It seems he is their only link. How can paper move him? Incredibly, his hand is shaking.

He rises; and holding his breath, for he has not paid the waitress or left a tip, he goes to the street where he calls down a cab with a wave and one loud whistle. He gets in and rides for a while. The engine has a smooth, cared-for sound, unusual in cabs. Whitaker loves cars and has owned a half dozen since his sixteenth birthday. He dreams of driving them now, one after the other, the Nash; the '52 Mercury; the Studebaker, which he hated; the Impala; the Fairlane.

Seen at first from afar, the monument to George Washington has an icy look. Yet it makes Whitaker think of a prick and he grins. Various mists and clouds move about the sky. They spread like stains. Whitaker, listening to the engine, envies the cabbie his cab. He loves his many bright memories of old roads and engine growls, gray old two-lane Wisconsin roads white with moonlight. His hands stir with what they recall of high-flying danger, the jolt that speed and shifting gears could create. For example, in a 1964 race at Langford in Tasmania, drivers blasted along at 170 mph in the rain. He was not there with them, but he did crack 110 mph on old Route 26. He has many such islands of knowledge that he visits as if they are somehow in his life. He thrills to the idea of these daredevils, the blur of their rush down those wet straights, like stones, flat as razors, skipping over a pond.

When the cab stops, Whitaker walks to the open driver-side window to pay. He cannot see into the mind of the man who is transfixed, lips slackened, eyes thin. He looks out fixedly at the thousands of people Whitaker takes in with a glance. They are noise and color, and the man, whose eyes seem to push Whitaker away, continues to sit there, staring even after Whitaker leaves.

I will only stay a little while, he thinks. I hate them, he thinks. The multitude flutters near the base of the Washington Monument. He moves toward them, but feels he is separate from them in a way larger than any length of grass across which he might walk. He occupies a hole deep in his mind where he tells angry jokes and conjures up the shapes of engines, wires, pipes, and pistons. These people would not understand. Not the wires or the jokes. He is with them today only because he woke and thought to come here. Because he thought he might learn of some way not to go to the war. Except that isn't true and he knows it. There'd been nowhere else for him to go. He might get a piece of ass. Some pussy. Some pleasure. He is a ghost among them. They demonstrate against the war, having taken a day to whoop and holler. But where is the war? They don't know that it's right there with them walking in their midst. They don't know that it has fallen with all its weight upon ole Whitaker. That he has its orders in his pocket. Papers that are like a chill and bony hand. He begins to whistle "Oh It's a Long Long Way to Tipperary" as he walks.

At a point to his right where the road curves around swells of grass leading toward the monument, he bumps into a surprising bunch of people distinguished from the others by their haircuts and clothing, their posters, their placards. They are the John Birchers, the Minutemen; and they have come to protest the protesters.

Dressed in his civilian clothes—his faded suit, polished shoes, white shirt, and pocketed tie—Whitaker feels they might mistake him for one of them, but he belongs to no one. I'm here to see what all this has to do with me, he thinks, and shoves his hands into his pockets. The mood of the place into which he is drifting is bright and cheerful. The John Birchers would despise him for not wearing his uniform, if they knew he had one, and the others, the hippies or beatniks or whatever they are, would despise him for even being in the service. He passes over neat grass toward a slab of road and the continuing grass beyond. White-suited vendors sell hot dogs and chestnuts from small, smoke-shrouded grills. He hunches his shoulders and cups his hands to protect a sparking match rising to his cigarette. A woman in a light blue suit is strolling toward him and staring intently to his right. She makes him think of Sharon, and then deny that he has thought of Sharon. The woman is not young, yet she is lovely. She would be interesting beneath him in this grass or in some dim room. Beyond her he sees a policeman talking from high on top of a black horse to a young boy and girl in pretty clothing: purple and yellow trousers, shirts printed with flowers. The policeman's black belt and blacker boots glitter, sharply. The woman in blue has gone past Whitaker. Watching her, he sees that she is what he wants in his mouth, not this cigarette, but her body beneath her clothing making him breathe harshly and think again of dark-eyed sweet Sharon who seems always a surprise when she proves that she can ambush him whenever she wants. He had thought her dismissed. He had not meant to want her anymore. He will never think to go to her again, he decides. He will seek some stranger first, any passerby. That woman in blue, where is she now? He doesn't know. He scarcely looks. Anyway, is this the only day in his life? There've been others. I'll get by. Who is Sharon? I'll get by. Bitterness gouges him in jagged bursts, like someone pounding nails. Anger, old and new, burns. It mixes with his stomach acid, with coffee and eggs and toast and the knowledge that in the days following the arrival of his orders he had wanted to howl. Now he blinks and the air and space and grass around him take him back. He sees himself alone and walking. He is on his way to the hospital to get his medical records. He is in an office where medics give him his brown folder of facts and three injections against foreign, creepy diseases. Vietnam, as an actual place and sinister force against him, begins to enter his brain with the bite of the needle entering his skin, passing through layers of tissue, touching his blood: bright alien piercing. His heart understands; it shudders; yet he has no sense of what has begun until he is outside and thinking strangely about that tree on the far side of the athletic field. He must drastically avoid it or something will happen. He must not hasten toward it. He must not press like a sickened man against it. He must not hug the black, thick trunk. As if his voice is vomit, he refuses to let it loose, while a beetle probes the creases in the bark beside his nose.

He is amid a cluster of trees across the road from the flat terrain of the mall and reflecting pool. Visible through foliage the Washington Monument stands, with people, like colorful snippets, gathering at its base. The policeman and his horse are plodding to the road where the woman in blue is looking confused. The young boy and girl are kissing. Her teeth touch his cheek. Whitaker, watching, feels envy and thinks how he was among the very first to come down on orders because a slim, fast-talking Irish New Yorker, Mickey Whalen, ass-kissed his way off those orders. Sleeping only a few bunks away in the same barracks as Whitaker, he brownnosed and ass-kissed a sergeant major who brownnosed and ass-kissed a captain who did the same to a major, and then the shit of it spread to a lieutenant colonel who sucked off a grinning, full, motherfucking colonel who had the orders amended—one name removed, another added. For the next few days everyone nodded at Whitaker and gave him sympathetic looks until one night, returning drunk from the post bowling alley, he pissed all over the sleeping Whalen, who jumped awake in startled disbelief, but did nothing more than stare while Whitaker weaved and towered over him, muttering and coughing and grunting until he was finally empty of his waste of beer and rage and piss.

I'm looking for something to happen, I want something to happen to me. He is fairly tall, a level six feet with a ruddy round face, thick chest and shoulders, straw-colored hair. I should go up to that woman and say something, some pleasant thing and then we could talk, and go for a beer, or dinner and then her place. I'd like someone. He hears himself thinking and stops. What does he mean? He lets his cigarette fall to the grass. A goateed man in a brown corduroy suit goes by, carrying a briefcase and striding with force and determination. Hatred flies out from Whitaker. A professor, probably, some teacher, some asshole.

Restless again, moving again, he looks around. The monument, very near now, strikes him as a harsher color, more the dull gray of cement. The lines of its three visible edges are like finely cut wires.

Ahead, the road toward which he ambles is lined by people bunched together in a meager space and wearing a mixture of ordinary clothing. He is surprised that the ranks of such regular citizens should contain so many police. Scattered among them are coffee urns and paper cups, an open picnic basket full of sandwiches wrapped in glittering aluminum foil. They chatter and laugh, displaying and elevating in no regimented way their sticks with tacked-on signs. BOYS ARE DYING IN VIETNAM THAT YOU MAY HAVE THE RIGHT TO PROTEST, reads one. REMEMBER HITLER AND 1938, says another. A young man in a red vinyl jacket dashes several paces forward before thrusting his slogan high: DO NOT FORGET POLAND. Behind him a slim girl, her hair piled up in thick blond curls, applauds and bounces up and down on the curb. Poland? thinks Whitaker. Two gleeful children, a boy and a girl, are stationed with a white banner at least ten feet long stretched between them. They both wear suits, hers with a skirt, his with pants, and the red letters of their message ripple in the breeze: IF YOU WANT TO BURN YOURSELF TO DEATH LIKE SOME GODLESS BUDDHIST WE HAVE THE GASOLINE FREE OF CHARGE! At the feet of each stands a red five-gallon fuel can. Within easy reach are other cans of differing sizes. Fumes, touched with sunlight, tremble above the lids.

Whitaker, rocking from foot to foot, thinks about going over to talk to the boy and girl. He sees himself in such an odd conversation, imagines, after a while, helping to hold up their banner. Then he sees himself drenching his own clothing with gas but cleverly burning the children instead. It makes him laugh. The crowd, in horror, tries to maul and destroy him. He flees in a Lotus-Ford.

A family is passing in front of him—five children, a mother and father—and all wear red, white, and blue paper hats and have big buttons pinned to their shirts that say war is unhealthy for children and other living things. The round, chubby father leads the way. The wife, a wobbly bird, carries a plaid picnic basket and nods, knowingly, at the father, who is saying, "I do, I do, let me tell you. I got the scars from shrapnel and other such bullshit all up and down my back."

"And your legs, too," she tells him, like she might know as much about it as he does.

Having no aim of his own, Whitaker falls in behind them. Their passing has a kind of steady suction. All together they turn, taking a slight upward detour before they turn again. Trailing along, Whitaker marches on toward a raised-up stage of dark wood set before rows of folding chairs, some metal, some wood. Ropes strung on poles driven into the ground form a perimeter. Policemen in teams man the several points of entry. Other cops pace the periphery or prowl among the chairs.

Whitaker looks eagerly about, hoping to learn the nature of the event into which he is entering. Clearly, he has happened upon something interesting, a destination toward which countless others are on the move, converging, like the spokes of a wheel toward their hub, which is the stage before which Whitaker has come to stand. People pass him in bunches large and small, their mingled conversations an unintelligible murmur. Nothing he overhears gives him a useful clue regarding where he is and what is about to happen. The policemen politely oversee the lines filing into the chairs. They seem unconcerned with the area Whitaker occupies. So he will stay there, steer clear of them. Stay out of their way. A cop walking by gives him a glance. Whitaker nods and turns away, as if any movement at all will help him find what he needs, and he bumps into something or someone. "Excuse me," he says, looking into the even brown eyes of a girl with endless lengths of strawberry hair braided into pigtails and decorated with two green ribbons.

"Sure," she says and starts away.

A button on the front of her colorful T-shirt admonishes him to make love not war. He thinks he might tag along.

"You know what's gonna happen here?" he says.

"What?"

"What's gonna happen here, you know?"

"A play."

"What do you mean?"

"You know, actors."

"What kinda play?"

She is eager to leave him; irritation and wariness come out of her, hurting his feelings. "I'm not sure I get it," he says.

"It's gonna be about the war. How it's bad, you know. I need to go, all right?"

"How it's bad?"

"You don't think it's good?"

"Oh. No."

"I mean, they're going to show it in the play, how it's immoral, more immoral than what the Nazis did to the Jews. That's what it will be about. I need to go, all right?"

"Sure. Fine."

"I'm looking for somebody," she says, and smiles, glancing back. "If you still don't know what you wanted ask one of the cops at those gates."

"All right. Fine," says Whitaker, and he wonders how she can just walk away without knowing that he is the one she is seeking. The one she has been seeking all her life. The perfect lay. Me, me, me, he thinks. Superprick. Your lover, your oiler. Let me grease you, baby, he thinks. Lay down in the grass, I'll grease your ass.

There's some sort of ruckus behind him. On the level wood of the stage a large furry figure has appeared. It is a man in an animal costume with the face of a bear or a gorilla, or so it looks to Whitaker, until he sees that it's not either, but a made-up face like that of a monster. The creature is moving about in the manner of someone looking for something lost and pretending to be unaware of all the watching eyes.

The body is not fur but scales, large clots of some hardened, plasterlike material. Having gotten nearer, Whitaker discovers that other creatures hover off to the side of the stage. His closeness gives him an angle to see them, though they would be hidden from the view of the people in the chairs. They clutch pistols, banners, swords, yet their postures are relaxed and conversational. He can't hear them, but can tell that they're chatting, casually, even cheerfully. Their eyes seem red scabs upon the boiled skin of their faces. Fangs pinch their purple lips. Their big noses have flared nostrils, like the nostrils of a snake.

Suddenly, the prowling creature removes its animal head,

revealing its human face. From somewhere unseen comes a beating drum. The creature wanders with no apparent purpose. One shrill trumpet cry floats on the noise of the drum. The red eyes of the many armed creatures hidden on the side move and fix upon the figure alone on the stage. But he does not notice. Whitaker knows what the play will be. The massed creatures will come shrieking out to drag the searching human one to the floor. In fierce pantomime, they will take his life with their fingerless hands. Whitaker pivots to leave, and the gray Washington Monument seems to have disappeared. It couldn't have moved. He jogs a short distance before a loud shout from behind pivots him to look back. A lectern has been placed at the center of the stage and behind it stands a man in a black suit, his hands pressed solemnly upon the upper edges of the lectern. As the costumed creatures collect in a semicircle behind him, the man lifts both pink hands into the air and also, it seems to Whitaker, into the tangle of treetops hanging behind the contours of the stage. Beneath these trees is a boxlike, light blue vehicle with lines of people at either end. Large letters printed on the side read: COMFORT STATION. Piss house, thinks Whitaker. Potty. Shit house. Poo-poo-pee-pee-ca-ca.

In a voice that hopes to possess the timbre of thunder, the power and danger of the almighty, the man behind the podium cries of god. The creatures stomp their feet and bang the butts of their weapons against the floor. Whitaker detests the unease he is feeling, the whisper of fear. Why is it there are so many here free yet he is a prisoner? None of them must go. They need not even know of his imminent departure. They are soft, disgusting people. Had they no hot dogs, he thinks, sullenly, no ice cream, no restrooms, no entertaining play to watch, they would not be here at all. He shakes his head and shakes it again. In this kind of heavy, evil mood he knows he must beware, because he can do vicious, destructive things even to himself. Two years ago, he leaped from his '52 Mercury, dented and steaming with water and oil beside the shattered telephone pole into which he had crashed. Scampering to the sidewalk he smashed his fists into the face of a startled bystander. For ninety-one days afterward, he slept on a hard bed in a jail cell under bars through which the city could be viewed only from on top of the shoulders of a fellow inmate. Sometimes overcrowding moved him into a cell block where crammed, restless prisoners milled, laughing, talking, telling stories. In sleep, they frowned and, dreaming, met their demons to whom they spoke, growling or crying out with choking sounds. Whitaker and Willy were the same age and of nearly the same build, and neither wanted to be touched by the queers thrown in from off the streets. They slept uncertainly and near each other. Then Willy was released, and three days later the ninetieth and final day of Whitaker's sentence went by, but no one came for him. The walls remained around him. Exhausted and frightened, he was seized by a brutal darkness of feeling and knowledge: he would never get out. He had disappeared and no one knew of him any longer. It was a feeling more awful than any he had ever known. Only lying facedown on his bunk with his teeth biting into his palms and his throat constricted by his refusal to sob or scream made him feel any better.

4

Standing among the curving, wrinkled trunks of palm trees, Lan is thinking of the ocean and Vung Tau's sandy shore. Her almond eyes are dark. The water is warm there. Buses make the forty-mile journey often. You pay your fare and then, if the VC stop you, there are taxes to be paid to them. Occasionally land mines blow up buses along the way, but these are mostly accidental. Does she have enough money? She would love to swim. To make such a trip by airplane would be a wonder. However, that is not a thing she can really hope for, though she does know a girl who claims to have flown. But the girl is a continual and foolish liar, and not out of politeness. She lies because she enjoys tricking people. But she is Chinese, and so her double-dealing is to be expected.

Lan wears many rings. She is thin and her hair is the blackness of the bottom of the sea piled high in plumes. Wind slightly stirs the palm fronds near her; they whisper and she is motionless. Now she is no longer thinking of the level blue acres of ocean at Vung Tau. Down the road that runs in from the fields before her a laboring, ponderous silhouette approaches, the thick-horned heads of water buffalo yoked together in wood. High on top of the wagon sits the farmer. Light yet lingers at the tip of the conical straw hat he wears. Low oblong shadows of pigs follow, while the shape of someone thin and short trails all, lifting now the length of the wooden staff. Lan's breathing falters with an alien, unwanted ache that makes her shake her head, touch two fingers to her brow; yet it continues within her, changing the expression of her eyes. Having ridden in such carts, she wants to be in one again. Her brother, now a Saigon taxi driver, had followed while her father drove. Their two pigs were bound to the wagon by wire attached to their right front feet; they rarely squealed; they struggled on their stubby legs to keep pace. Her brother, Linh, prodded their flabby flanks with a bamboo stick, which he sometimes flourished above his head as if it were a sword. In the daylight it flashed yellow; under the moon it seemed white. Brandished swiftly, a whistling sound sprang from it into the air. And all along the dike walls were flowers that she sometimes picked and took with her father to the family altar covered with pictures of ancestors and strange holy men from other countries. There were drawings and symbols of her many dead relatives. And then one day a picture of her father was placed among them, along with the shirt he had worn on the day of his death. Still it lies there, she knows, seeing the slack cloth, as black as soil. Do his eyes see her now? she wonders. Waking one morning, sweating and dizzy, illness clearly in his eyes, he went out into the fields to work.

Sometime in the afternoon, with no one watching, he toppled sideways into a few feet of water and the buffalo halted beside him. Probably he struggled once or twice to his knees, where he rested and then fell again. In the end he lay there drowning, too weak to call out or lift himself, while the animals stood as they had been trained, awaiting further commands.

She brought no flowers to the shirt. The shirt was not there when she brought the flowers. She was a child bringing flowers, and a girl when the drowning of her father left the shirt to lie useless upon the altar. She studied it lying there once each day for a week before she finally wept, though she had pretended weeping at the funeral.

Her breathing is slow. Her mind and breath repeat the rhythms of her blood and pulses. Down a final streak of daylight a bat falls steeply, wings poised. It seems to strike something hidden in the air and then, turning sideways and upward, it flees for the forest where the night is already deep. As if those cool wings have brushed against her, she shudders, but only once, beginning to smile, still staring and thinking, repeating again the memory of it all: a mother, a father, a brother, three sisters, and a farm. What of the rumored generations of her ancestors, the watching dead of her blood? The line of her smile lengthens. To think of them makes the air seem alive with eyes all fixed on her. No, she is too small for such concern. Nearly invisible, she is too faint to ever be so exactly known and observed. Monthly she sends money to her mother and sisters. She hopes this is her only meaning to the dead. She has turned and begun to walk, her head moving from side to side. Little, she thinks, can be demanded from little. She feels comforted.

The car wash is empty now. For a moment, from the doorway, she examines the emptiness, a space of air like smoke bound by the dull stone of the walls. Why the GIs ever come, she doesn't know, but they do: with hungers and money and noise and an eagerness to have her that, when they are not cruel, bewilders her and puts her into fits of helpless laughter. They think her of such enormous value.

She prowls the room, the dirt-stained tile of the floor. A gecko darts and stops. Her feet are small in her worn-out slippers, and reaching the front doorway, her eyes seek into the night, the road before her thudding with a huge green truck caked with wrinkled dust, loaded with crates. The sink and surge of the pavement comes through the earth to her feet. Then the cab and trailer vanish with a rush and before her the glowing fields wave across the road. With nearly no sound at all, an ancient, rust-colored man drifts past on his whispering bicycle, his head bowed under his conical hat, as if he rides in his sleep. Children appear at the edge of the field. Lan's nose wrinkles with the start of a sneeze, and she goes out and heads back past Madame Lieu's house and the other shanties, some of tin, others of wood and straw. From the deep stone hollowness and glitter of a well, she hauls up water. She sheds her yellow, silky pajamas. The water flickers and slaps as she pours the bucket into a dented gray pan. Alone and unthinking under the bright stare of the moon, she splashes and scrubs her skin, which seems to her aglow. Only the black of her hair would be invisible, a piece of the night. And she is singing, brief starts and stops of a song that frolics, possessing both sadness and gaiety, and she is back in the wilds again, younger, returned to the forest streams.

With a bright fluff of cloth she rubs herself dry. With a feeling of newness, she fits herself into her scarlet padded bra and scarlet underwear, plain cotton pajamas, and sandals of a pleasant mahogany leather.

Back toward the road in a second stone house lives Madame Lieu, the owner of the car wash. Lan will go there now for her money. The water, dumped from the pan, rushes through a cluster of small stones before collecting finally upon a hard flatness of ground. Calling to Madame Lieu, Lan pivots and enters a room crowded with debris. A chicken squawks and struts from beneath the wreckage of a bicycle stacked against a wall. Madame Lieu is old and the clothing she wears is a shabby brown. She spits, and shows her teeth with their rusty, nearly blackish stain, for she chews incessantly upon the leaves of the betel nut tree. This discoloration of teeth was once thought a mark of beauty in the women of Vietnam. Girls went through a long and uncomfortable process so their teeth would darken and men would think them beautiful. But it is no longer done. Lan, personally, finds it repulsive and old-fashioned. Even though the old women say there is delight in the juices, Lan would never want her teeth to be that ugly color. Almost no young girls do it any longer.

Shoulders bowed, an indentation creasing her shirt down the length of her spine, Madame Lieu has the look of a cripple, though she is not, having endured, Lan knows, nearly fifty years. Lan requests her money. The woman nods, offering a bowl of rice and sauce, bits of dried fish. Gratefully, Lan crosses to the huge steaming kettle scorched black in its bed of simmering coals. The glow touches redness to her mouth, chin, even the tip of her nose, while her eyes glisten like a liquid darker than the shadows the embers cast. Filling the bowl, she settles on a small worn bench and begins to eat, scooping the food with chopsticks, the bowl held close to her mouth. Madame Lieu is slouched on a stool nearby. She strikes a match to light a cigarette. In an un-steady voice, she whispers that she is tired, but her son is doing well in school, though they will come for him soon, the army, the draft. She heard, recently, from a friend who has a brother who is a policeman in Bien Hoa that the police will be coming to Tan Mai soon, next month more than likely. Proceeding from house to house, they will seek out and take the young men.

Lan nods, listening. Madame Lieu is frowning, sitting rigidly and downcast in her worry and silence. Wind, carrying a degree of chill, brushes past them; the embers glow more extremely, the heat increasing, and the shapes of the shadows change. Faint in the distance are the cries of children, the rumble of trucks. The coals crackle, their strength waning. The gloom, mottled with dust, grows deeper. Lan stands up. She sets the white bowl upon the table, then passes softly across the room to Madame Lieu who hands her the crumpled bills of five hundred and fifty piastres. Lan nods, saying nothing more, departing. Madame Lieu calls farewell after her and Lan, stepping lightly along the path between the houses, responds.

When the road is before her, she scurries to the far side where the weeds are thicker, and barbed wire, sprung loose from the stakes about which it was bound, juts out at peculiar angles. The immense sky is nearly cloudless. Waiting for a Lambretta taxi to take her home, she stands awhile. The traffic is heavy, headlights and noise bringing American army and air force trucks and jeeps booming past. Some rush toward Bien Hoa while others bounce by in the opposite direction, heading toward Long Binh and the growing army compound there. Lambretta taxis sputter and shake along, their rear cabs like big crates stuffed with GIs in fatigues or civilian clothes. They yelp at her in their vulgar, incomprehensible language, gesturing out the sides with their hands about fuck-fuck and suck-suck. Every now and then one of them will call out in clumsy Viet-

namese. She practices aloofness before them, surrendering neither look nor sound, thinking to herself how they will believe
her innocent and ignorant, a child. She is grinning at this when
she hears her name called in a voice that is Vietnamese. Doan
Tan Kim, a girl of twelve who lives with her parents next door
to Madame Lieu, is running up from her home toward the
road. The child's face is round, eyes eager, as she is asking if
Lan will please accompany her to the Bien Hoa cinema; she
can go if Lan will take her.

Lan waves her hands, crying out, No, no, she cannot go;
she hasn't time. No time, no time. Yet there is laughter in her
voice, and pleasure also.

"Please."

"I have been forbidden, for I have VD. No VD in the movies."

"No one knows."

"I don't even know. Only the GIs know."

"What?"

"They yell and worry."

"Please."

"What is VD? Kim, do you know?"

"Please, please."

"Only if you take me, Kim. You must take me," says Lan,
bending to the child as if to explain a mysterious, complicated
procedure.

"But you are the oldest. You must take me."

"But I cannot even go unless you take me, and you won't, so
how can I take you? Don't you see?"

"Oh."

"Yes."

"All right, yes," says Kim.

"So will you take me, Kim, please?"

"If you promise to be good."

"I promise."

"No GIs," Kim says.

"If they talk to me, I will look the other way. I will hide my eyes."

"That will only make them chase you. You must be ugly."

"I am ugly."

"All right."

"I will tell them I have a fish in my pussy."

"Yes."

"I will tell them I have piss in my pussy."

"A fish to bite them."

"VD. Shit. What is the movie?"

The Lambretta taxi that finally halts to allow them to squeeze aboard is crammed with scraps of damp, sweet-smelling lumber of a whitish color. Between two fingers, Lan pinches shut her nose and exchanges a delighted grin with Kim. The Lambretta sways into motion, grinding gears, squeaking. Lan closes her eyes. "I think," she says, "we must try to be luckier in the life we have after this one."

"I think so, yes," Kim says.

"We will be men."

"Yes."

"Very big."

"Important."

"Americans."

"Americans."

"And we will come to Vietnam."

"Yes, yes." Kim is giggling; she stomps her tiny feet, covering her mouth with her fingers. "I think you are crazy."

"No, no, I am too pretty to be crazy."

"But you are ugly, remember?"

"Yes, yes. One minute one thing and then something else."

The shapes of huts, like wayward shadows not quite ready for the ground, float past them in the dark. There is the steady whirring of the Lambretta motor carrying them along.

Kim says, "I don't know why you talk so crazy."

"It is a mystery."

"Didn't you say just before that you were ugly?"

"That was before. A joke. Why do you think the GIs want me if I am not pretty?"

"Because they are crazy."

"You think they are crazy, too?"

"Yes."

"You think everybody is crazy."

"Yes."

"Well, you are half right. They are crazy. But I am pretty."

Downtown Bien Hoa is a spangling of many lights—beacons, drifting crowds and cries, figures darting—men, women, girls, bikes, and children. Suddenly, the slumbering communities along the road are gone and the city, Bien Hoa, has sprung up on them, huge and dissonant. Lan laughs at the sight of it all. Soldiers of many kinds of armies and races plunge into bar after bar. Here the girls wear wonderful clothing; their hair is done in beauty parlors and they outsmart the GIs. If they are beautiful, they fool and beat the GIs. Drinking tiny glasses of tea, they lie, they promise impossible enchantments; and then the drunken GIs wander off to fuck-fuck with old ugly women while the young girls are free to pick who they want, or to just make money. She wishes fiercely that she had the will, the audacity, and the shamelessness to come here to work, to come to Bien Hoa to work and win.

The cinema lies ahead. Lights are brilliant there. The square before it is a marketplace of teeming shops and stalls. A billiard hall stands adjacent to it with its big windows full of men and boys moving through a gray mix of cigar, pipe, and cigarette smoke in the bright yellow shimmer spilling onto the street. The Lambretta bounces to a halt. After paying the driver, Lan and Kim scamper hand in hand over a path that winds among the shops. Springing up the final steps, pausing only for tickets, they enter the theater, a sudden crackling gloom through which they move stealthily. Lan's face reflects light from the radiant screen showing a valley of rolling green beyond which towers a range of mountains peaked in whiteness. Kim's hand within Lan's own seems exquisite. Down from the high hills leap horsemen, who, because of the oiled blackness of their hair and the texture of their skin, seem Vietnamese, though they whoop and holler in French, and the audience shouts, "VC! VC!" while across the base of the screen come the printed words of what they are saying.

5

Whitaker is in a bar where he drinks and mopes, unable to lift himself from the dark mood into which he has fallen. Rage keeps him in danger of telephoning Sharon for nearly an hour, his throat tight with hatred of her and the words he would shout. But he doesn't do it, because finally an idea comes along that's smart enough to stop him: he asks himself if it's really Sharon he wants or is "Sharon" merely the only name he knows in Washington for what he wants? With this thought, he understands at last, and the sensation frees him to smile and decide to return to the mall and the flower children there. She has chosen another, married another—let it be, let it be—though to mess up their marriage as his last stateside act would be a real pleasure.

In his right-hip pocket, he carries a newly purchased pint flask of whiskey, silver and insulated, and the cap, when removed, is precisely the measure of a shot glass. Eagerly, he journeys by bus and on foot back to the mall. He hastens along, certain he will find a girl among the thousands here; maybe the one with pigtails will reappear, or the woman in blue—there are so many—or just one who notices him as he is noticing her.

Sauntering along, eyeing this one and that one, he passes a parked bus and comes upon a gigantic swastika. Black and red and as huge as a billboard, the draped flag covers the side of a semitruck trailer illuminated in the failing afternoon by floodlights. He realizes that for the past few minutes he has been ignoring an electronically amplified voice disjointed by static. Loudspeakers stand at either end of the roof of the trailer. In barks and spurts they broadcast a garbled version of whatever the slim man positioned at a microphone is saying. Like the sturdy guards on either side of him, the man is dressed in a Nazi Brownshirt uniform. Similar figures occupy the rooftop or stand in a line on the grass in front of the trailer. Many hold upraised placards that proclaim support for the boys in Vietnam. Everyone has a swastika armband. The generator powering the lights gives off an uncertain motorized grumble. The man raps on the microphone, sounding annoyed and suspicious as he declares, "Testing, one two three."

A slim young man in a navy pea coat and two leggy girls in cowgirl-style coats with beaded satchels slung over their shoulders are departing as he approaches. One of the girls tilts her head at Whitaker, and he turns to watch her go, but she pays no further attention. When he looks back, he is surprised by the troop of policemen in black, hip-length leather coats hurrying up. They form a line along the front of the trailer.

They are amazing. He has a sudden vision of the cops and Nazis fighting. They pound and shoot one another. He cheers them on. Six of the police wear soft hats; two have helmets. One is a black, a captain with thick legs stuffed into knee-high boots.

Whitaker lights a cigarette and puffs away, excitedly, his hands in his pockets, shoulders hunched. The mechanical problem with the loudspeakers must have been solved because he's able to hear the man cough and then, as if easy-going and friendly, say, "If you can argue with me, argue. If you can tell me that I'm wrong, I'll listen, but you just mill about like cows."

There is the bellow of a human imitating a cow.

". . . You offer no response but sarcasm. Having no intelligence, you defend yourselves with sarcasm. Nonsense." Stomping his foot, the man pivots. His blond-haired thin body disappears down a trapdoor in the roof of the trailer. His replacement, popping up almost immediately, is dark and thickly built, with narrow eyes set in deep sockets that hold him back from the world at a remote and careful distance. Yet he is young; there is about him the animal vitality of a good high school athlete, a hard-nosed football player, maybe a guard, grown only a few years older.

"Peace creeps," he says, grinning. "Our day is coming, you bunch of dirty yellow nigger-loving peace creeps."

Someone near Whitaker lifts his voice in loud protest that fades into, "Says you!" The young Nazi continues to grin, looking down with pitying eyes upon the ignorance gathered before him.

"We're going to take a little break now," he says. "I'll be gone for a while."

Two or three cheers arise, bringing on laughter.

Still, no tension shows in the young man's voice or stance. "And when I come back," he says, reassuringly, "we'll have a leader of the Ku Klux Klan give a little talk and Herb 'The Skull' Booker of the L.A. chapter of Hell's Angels has some things he wants to say to you peace creep commie bastards and if we're lucky, George Lincoln Rockwell, who is at this moment in the dirt of one of the commie peace creep jails of this city, suffering for his heroism, his inability to stand still in the face of the insult of a red Cong Commie flag being waved in the air of the streets of America. And he tore it from their hands, spit on it, and for that crime he was hauled off by the misguided flunkie police of the misguided white officials of this great city, thrown into jail, a hero, George Lincoln Rockwell, who if freed before this day is out, and if certain of the mood and merit of this crowd, will come here to speak to you."

A group of people standing directly in front of the big swastika count from one to three and deliver a loud and coordinated, "Booo!" The young Nazi's voice changes, shrillness entering somewhere into it, even though the pleasant, friendly smile remains. "And he will say the truth into your sweet faggot peace-creep nigger-loving ears."

As his predecessor vanished, so he also drops from sight through the trapdoor. Loud, raw sounds of music replace him, a guitar and chimes, a group of male voices in a folksy style, homey and amiable, singing with wonder and happiness of the bells that will ring and ring, the shouts of triumph and joy, when the white man's day has come:

> "'We're gonna load those ships
> Gonna wave farewell,
> Gonna get those apes back in those trees,

Gonna send those niggers back,
Gonna send those niggers back.'"

Whitaker yells, "Can we keep Willie Mays?" He takes a big drink of whiskey. "Willie Mays won't do Africa no good. They'll never win the World Series." Herb "The Skull" Booker, he thinks. He likes the nickname. Ku Klux Klan—all these men in white sheets. George Lincoln Rockwell. It feels like a goddamn circus, and to have the whiskey at his finger-tips is luxurious, the fulfillment of his wish given as he asks for it. Giddiness comes flying at him. While at the bar he downed a number of shots and beers, and though his capacity is large, he has eaten little. He is slipping forward past random figures, while the singing fades. Sudden martial music squalls into the graying air, the drums and brass of the armies of the Third Reich. Weaving to the very front of the crowd, Whitaker finds that he is staring into the brown, shiny face of the black po-lice captain. The man stands without expression, as blank and mute as a stone, as if nothing moves in his brain, and he has not even heard the music, the singing, the words. Willy, Whita-ker's only sure friend in jail, was black. It was Willy who gave him the word about calling Negroes "blacks," and it was to Jones, another black guy, that he went with his dumb grief at his loss of Sharon. Not even three days since his last evening with her, he trudged up the concrete stairs to his barracks, leav-ing behind the phone booth where he'd just called her. Down the aisle of bunks and lockers he went until he stood in front of Jones's bunk, noticing for the first time the pinkness of the soles of those brown feet. He communicated his wish for Jones to follow him down to the porch. Jogging quietly, Whitaker crossed to the field between the barracks and the parking lot of the post shopping center. He felt thin in the emptiness and oddly singular, turning to shout to Jones, who was taking his time. Sharon was married—she'd gotten married, Whitaker yelled, his voice delivering his disbelief and hurt more fully than the facts he meant to be stating. Jones chuckled and went back inside.

"How about you," says a voice. "You." A Nazi is speaking. The eyes above the moving lips are fixed on Whitaker. "Yeah, yeah," he says.

"What?"

"Let's talk. Comeer. Comeer."

A young black guy, thin and wearing colorful clothing, is close by, dancing and nervous, turning constantly, nibbling his fingers.

"You interested in the organization?"

"This?" Whitaker says.

"The Nazi Party. I saw you come to the front of the crowd."

"This here the recruitin' sergeant, man," the black guy says. "You watch out he don't git you. He don't talk to me. How come is that, Sergeant?"

The Nazi, smiling, turns to look at the black guy.

"I'd be awful damn pretty in one a those suits you wearin', man, awful pretty," the black guy says. He looks at Whitaker. "They want you 'cause you blond, so you be more fun." The words swarm on his tongue, a hint of hysteria in their speed, and a hint of some danger in the gleam in his eyes, the bitterness in his laughter.

"How 'bout it?" the Nazi says.

"Let him be," says the black guy.

Something lives between them, an emotion, or energy, as if the black guy has taken up a dare and to win he must keep close to the Nazi, like a man terrified of snakes poking with a rake, a cane, a pencil into the sleeping coils of a cobra.

"Because I'm black is the answer," he says. "Because I ain't white."

"Because you're not human."

His response is strictly tension; his lips move and his tongue flicks to make a sound, but only air rushes out.

"You know that," the Nazi tells him.

Whitaker has turned, he is leaving.

"Where you going?" the Nazi calls.

"He gone, man," says the black guy. "You lose him."

"C'mon back here."

"Good-bye, man; good-bye."

Whitaker strides against the grain of the crowd. It is the last Saturday of his final free weekend and he is walking about in the cold of a fading winter day like a man with all the time he could ever wish for. When he has no time at all, no real time. And money is time and he has thirty-eight dollars. He knows what he wants, a girl, a lush red room, the money to buy the wealth of both, the happiness of her body, wine bottles on the night table; he wants a gorgeous slut like those he saw endlessly passing by him on the arms of braying and balding buyers and sellers of the world as he huddled two years ago in the hotel vestibule with the two or three others who earned their living, as he did, parking rich men's cars in Milwaukee, where he'd gone to try something different, get a taste of big city life. It was there that his draft notice found him. Shit, he thought. And then somebody told him he could get training as a mechanic. Most people had never even heard of Vietnam or a possible war at the time. He sure hadn't. He was twenty. So why the hell not?

Carburetor, he thinks, mixes the right amount of gas with the right amount of air to get combustion. In a six-cylinder engine, how does the spark go from cylinder to cylinder? One. Five. Three. Six. Two. Four. What's it get you? He doesn't know. He has no answer. For all his questions there has been no answer given to him ever; and now he is alone and nearly drunk and afraid that if he goes to Vietnam, he will die there.

Though aware for several instants of the three figures approaching, he has resisted thinking about them explicitly. Now he glances right and left to determine whether they have been spied by a consequential number of any of the others in the crowd. Above the three heads flutters a rectangle of red and blue cloth carried on a pole. The last of the whiskey is sweet on his tongue and he can barely believe his first conclusion, which is that the cloth is a Vietcong flag. They look like high school kids, skinny, all wearing glasses. Acne is so extreme on the face of one it seems the scars from some awful burn. They are punks, Whitaker thinks. He can see it in the way they walk—the diaries they keep, the mothers they worship, the altars of sweet kindness and good virtue at which they think they mean to lay their lives.

He hears a thump, a stumble. Someone flies past him. Colliding in sudden struggle, a squat, sturdy man with a Nazi armband pulls at the flag clutched in the hands of two of the three boys, the third having scampered away. There are gasps, grunts, and curses. Then a police paddy wagon, inert and silent till now at the curb, winds up with a roar. Its light goes on and spins. Distant parts of the crowd splinter and move in bits and pieces toward the commotion, where they reassemble in a murmuring, excited circle around the violence.

Locked in a tussle with the two youths, his fury splitting his mouth open, the Nazi howls as he is overwhelmed from behind by the dark mob of police who pinion his arms to his sides and grab his flailing legs while he screams, "George Lincoln Rockwell! America!"

From the roof of the trailer behind Whitaker comes the voice of the all-American-looking moderator: "The man is a hero. Like their leader, that man and the others who follow all believe in America. Who out here does not feel hatred for these commie flunkie bastard kids?"

"Yeah," yells Whitaker. He shakes his fist. He doesn't know what he's doing.

At the curb now, the shackled body of the Nazi clatters into the back of the paddy wagon.

The teenagers have regrouped. They are examining the crowd building around them, pride and excitement ignited in their eyes. Whitaker, watching, grimaces and wants a big drink but his flask is empty. He tilts his head way back, managing to coax a few drops down his throat. It's clear now that these kids plan to march directly over to the Nazi trailer waving their enemy flag. He hates them. He has known them and hated them all his life, the bookworms, the grade-A brown-nosing teacher's pets with chemistry sets in their basements, shortwave radios tuned to nowhere, and telescopes trained out their attic windows onto the moon. Because they have been told they are special, they think that the flag they carry is the flag of honor and decency because they carry it. It's you you love, you pricks, thinks Whitaker as the three of them start off. They expect to be followed. They expect that everyone who sees them will helplessly fall in behind them. This belief is on their faces, in their eyes, and so no one is prepared for the second man who leaps at them, snatching the banner and running with it over the grass. For an instant it appears he might make it to the road where he will have a chance, if the driver of the car parked there with its engine running is in fact an accomplice. Then he stumbles, staggers, falls, and scrambling up, churns straight into the waiting arms of the black police captain. Bone hits bone. A cry goes up from the crowd. The flag falls loose. The two figures wrestle to a kind of standstill and fall over. They roll from shade to better light. This man wears no uniform, no swastika. Some of the spectators demand his release. He starts squirming to get free of this lone cop before reinforcements, who can be seen and heard rushing closer, arrive. The black captain has his nightstick across the chest of the man. With one hand clenching either end he strains inward to hold the man who is really a teenager, kicking and twisting but making no cry. Then there is an instant of relaxation as the policeman attempts to adjust his grip. When the teenager slackens his legs, trying to drop straight down to get loose, the black captain recovers and the stick drives inward to recapture the kid, but because his head has lowered to where his chest used to be, the club smashes into his face. Blood explodes, a startling, bright, almost fakeseeming quantity and color. The kid is instantly quiet, sinking onto his hands and knees, where he freezes, as if to wait quietly until all danger passes.

Then he vomits and falls over.

"Get out," one of the cops is saying and pointing at the teenagers. "Get out, you sonsabitches."

"We don't have to," says the tallest, the leader.

"Get out," the cop says.

"You peace creep commie flunkies," says Whitaker, grinning and giddy. "I came here to have a good time. I ain't had no good time."

The voice of the Nazi moderator calls loudly, suddenly, "Do you want to hear George Lincoln Rockwell? Do you want him to speak?"

"Fuck no," yells some member of the crowd.

"Get out," the cop says.

"Bunch a phonies," says Whitaker.

"Shut up," says a cop, pointing at Whitaker.

"Not me," says Whitaker as the cop, with a companion, begins to advance upon him. "Okay," he says, "okay," his hands up.

"George Lincoln Rockwell will speak to you if you wish," says the moderator. "All you need to do is let him know that you wish it!"

The generator fails. For a minute the sputtering of its confusion is audible while the floodlights illuminating the moderator dim, tremble, flare up, and go dark. Cheering erupts from a small part of the crowd, but most are barely attentive any longer, beginning to leave. Dusk is thickening, the chill fall of evening nearly upon them. The victim, the kid who went for the banner, is slumped limply against the rear-left fender of the paddy wagon, a handkerchief, leaking blood, pressed against his slack mouth.

On top of the trailer a thin shadow, the young Nazi, lifts both arms toward the sky, each finger straining to its farthest extension, and his voice, when it comes, is small and human, crying after them, stripped of the distortion of the speaker system: "George Lincoln Rockwell will speak to you if you wish him to. All you need to do is let him know. Just let him know you will be receptive. Make your feelings known. What do you wish?"

He is staring out at them, a tilted silhouette pressing heavily forward, hands clutching the rod of the microphone stand, and there is about him some sense of enormity, weight, and thought.

"You fucking peace creep bastards," he says, addressing the spaces of lawn and wind. He shakes his head as if to shed a burden. And when he begins to shout now, it is not without the eerie trace of intelligence and humor, the unexpected awareness in his voice of the grade-B movie tyrants he is playing, the Capones and Neros stripped of all but fury. There's slyness, too, the startling surprise of wit in his fanatic brain: "We've got your names and pictures. Remember that. We know who you are. We've got your names on a list. Nineteen seventy will be the year. Think of it. Dream of it. We've got your fingerprints, names and addresses, the names of your brothers and sisters, parents and children. We'll come for you. Nineteen seventy."

Whitaker walks away, and he keeps going until the reflecting pool stretches out in a dull gleam alongside him. Looking back he can see where he was only moments ago. The trailer remains with shapes bustling about. Whitaker turns to continue on. Forty or fifty yards to his right, a slight roll in the terrain levels out quickly. A swatch of red catches his eye and he sees a blanket with two youthful figures beginning, at the instant he is aware of them, to crawl about gathering up their belongings. A radio plays pop music. The blond head of the girl bounces and wavers to the changes in the sounds.

"These are my orders," he says, hurrying toward them holding out his piece of mimeographed paper. The boy, on one knee, is stuffing books into a leather bag. "These are my orders," Whitaker whispers into their bewilderment. The girl is looking inquiringly at the boy. Can he explain? Does he know this stranger?

"I have to go. I have orders," says Whitaker.

"What do you mean?"

"I have to go."

"Do you mean the war?" The boy speaks softly, his voice very cultured, graceful.

"I'm in the army," Whitaker says.

"They can't make you go."

"Let me screw your girl," Whitaker says. "Okay?"

"What?"

"C'mon."

"What?"

"She's a flower child, isn't she? A love child, isn't that right? I'll give you a dollar. Let me dick her."

"Hey, c'mon, man."

"C'mon what?"

The boy looks to the girl. Whitaker looks, too, and her eyes are big and then they narrow.

"I'll give you two dollars; ten dollars; twelve; the keys to my car. All my money."

"No," the boy says. "I'm sorry."

"I ought to bust you up, that's what I ought to do. I want to. I want to bust in your face. I don't know why I'm not, you god-damn pussy. You jerk. You stupid jerk. You're just lucky, you know that? I want to break you apart just because of how you look, that's what I want more than anything. You baby-boy jerk. Do you know how lucky you are?"

He is crouching to look coldly into the boy's eyes, so his gaze is as huge as the threat of his coiled body.

The girl is staring in horror.

"Yes," the boy says. "I do."

"That's right."

"Yes."

6

As the first movie nears its ending, Lan tells Kim to guard her place while she goes for some snacks. Kim nods without looking away from the screen, and Lan hastens up the aisle littered with straw, bits of paper, sticks from cubes of sugarcane. She moves with her head bowed, as if in actual fear that her small body might interfere with the flow of the projector light that burns at the rear of the theater and streams through coils of smoke to deliver the image of big white wagons wobbling up a hillside. In the vestibule, she asks the usher to please remember her face because she does not want to have to pay on her way back in. He says he will remember her perfectly if she brings him a little snack, too. She gives him a quick look of exasperation, a brief, bright roll of her eyes, before going on down the stone stairs to the many stalls of wood and tin with their wooden benches and counters of food. Her appetite, at the sight of it all, doubles. She purchases a bowl of rice with fish and pork sauce, which she will eat hurriedly before getting three of some kind of fruit, one each for Kim, the usher, and herself. Studying the colorful displays glistening under the streetlamps, she begins to scoop the rice to her mouth, deciding upon oranges. She will order three and have them placed in a brown paper sack to make them easier to carry. Or maybe she will have grapefruit. Or maybe mango shoots. The stalls are innumerable, their odor intense and luscious, all the hundred wonderful thousand things in the world to eat.

Above the bright lights of the market, the sky is a strange color. The moon shudders and the sky wavers. The voice of the marketplace fades. Clouds ripple like fingers. The vendor hands her three oranges. Did she ask for them? Did she pay? He counts out her change and walks away. The bowl she ate from sits empty on the counter. She peels one orange, slowly, waiting. The vendor looks back at her and seems to be waiting, too. She sees that he is missing an arm, his left arm. The knotted sleeve dangles, and his eyes are still on her.

The man understands that the girl with the orange has no idea that she reminds him of his dead daughter now gone more than a year. It's that long since ARVN troops battled Vietcong to control his village, Binh Gia. Qui and two of her brothers, Than and Bao, were killed as fiery bombs devoured people. The rockets and mortars fell everywhere. But he has customers waiting, a young couple with a crying baby.

Lan senses that the man is about to look away. She feels a puzzling sadness, a kind of tender rebuke. Who is he? Should she know him? She smiles and gestures, as if to ask these question, but she isn't certain he sees, and then he's back at work.

7

Sharon's apartment, as he stands before it, is darkened windows over which the shades are silently drawn. He waits, though the rapping of his knuckles on the door has ceased. The stillness makes him hear a wind in the park across the street. They spent a Sunday morning seated on a bench there, he and Sharon; they rested through the quiet hours, reading a Sunday paper, trading the various sections, sharing occasional comments; each had been pleasantly at ease and accepting of the other and the silence. Now there comes a ticking from within the wood of the walls of the building before him. He waits, knocks again; no one comes; no one is home; she is not at home.

He crosses to the park where there is a phone booth from which he calls into the midwest to speak to his father. Initially, he has difficulty making the apparatus accept his dime, but eventually, he raises an operator who asks for more money, and then there comes the buzzing of the distant ringing in the big old house in which both his father and brother live. He has a moment's vision of the flat expanse of frosted, brittle land surrounding the few buildings of the farm, the barn and sheds, the house itself, three stories tall. Each blade of grass and weed is singly frosted. He hears the ringing within that house, glowing in his imagination as if he is nearby instead of wandering the various pathways, cinder and concrete, of this park in Washington, D.C. Suddenly, he hangs up the phone to stand as still as a listening hunter who has heard the noise of the animal he must kill.

Through a webbing of black tree limbs and changing wind, Sharon is the object of a consuming concentration. Dressed in an aqua suit, boots, and light-colored net stockings, she is on the steps that rise from the sidewalk to the door. He ducks behind a tree. She has her keys. The door slams shut.

Walking briskly, he returns to the bar where he has been drinking. He sits on the bar stool, his feet tucked onto the lower rungs, for he is free at last of her power to make him grieve because she, who was requisite to his life, is gone. But she is not requisite. She is not air, not oxygen. She is not breath. Empty of her now, the expanse of his imagined future grows enormous. He can go to any girl. He downs a shot of Seagram's whiskey followed by a beer. To celebrate, he orders another pair of drinks, and feeling himself already present in his new and limitless life, he goes to the jukebox that is all glass and glitter like a jewelry case. Sealed away below him are miniatures of the covers of top-selling albums, rotating like small carousels. He leans nearer to see more clearly the delight of their colorful design, and his dog tags, clinking one against the other, make a sound that falls like a cannon down his mind. He freezes, his fingers pressed upon the glass. Only yesterday he read a letter sent from 3rd Platoon, ALPHA Company, 3rd Battalion, 1st Infantry Division. It was monsoon season, said the letter. The mud was deep. There was no end to it, no place where it was not. He read of huge rats that crept into camp each night in search of garbage. The heat was constant. He learned of spooky black nights. There was no moonlight in a jungle, said the letter, and so the dark was total in which tiny yellow people probed the concertina wire for flaws through which to pass to go among the sleeping men, setting charges of plastic explosives, or with the speed of a snake's head striking, cutting one white sleeping throat.

Whitaker frowns and fingers his dog tags. They tell him who he is and he squints, remembering the letter's final page, which told of one day at dawn when a boy, clumsy with sleep, triggered the trap of a bomb set at the ends of the straddle trench where he was squatting to shit. The explosion threw his ragged chest and head and arms into the pit, where he shuddered, eyes wide and monstrous in his huge distress. Some nights tracers swept in from the jungle, coming low and dangerous, until they reached the limit of their thrust, where they tumbled unnoted into the foliage or dirt.

Goddamn, says Whitaker, goddamn, and beneath the glass under his fingers a cardboard face of pert Petula Clark goes floating by.

8

"Fisher here," says the voice over the phone.

"Hello," Whitaker says.

"Yes, please."

"May I speak to Sharon?"

"May I ask who is calling please?"

"I'm Joe Whitaker."

"Sharon's married now, you know."

"Yeah, I heard that."

"I'm her husband, Bob Fisher, Joe. Could I take a message? Sharon's in the shower."

"Oh."

"Is there a message?"

"I'm just an old friend is all and I'm in the army and I've got to ship out next week, a week from today, as a matter of fact . . . overseas . . . Vietnam . . . , actually. So I just thought it might be nice if I could say hello. I'd like to meet you, too. I've been in town all day."

"It's awfully late."

"What time is it?"

"It's late."

"Somewhere around eleven."

"It's nearer twelve, Joe. Look at your watch."

"I didn't think it would matter since it's Saturday. I didn't get you up, did I?"

"No."

"Well, would it be all right maybe if I called back in maybe ten minutes? Would she be out of the shower by then, do you think?"

"Wait a minute; she's out now."

Of course, he thinks.

"Hang on."

And so he settles deeper into the confinement of that sweaty booth, wondering if she's naked and twinkling with beads of light and water at the top of the stairs. Or is she wrapped in a towel, held in a robe? Was she in any shower? Muted through the panels encasing him in wood and Plexiglas come the murmuring voices, the music of the taproom crammed with people, where smoke hangs and shifts like currents. The glass of beer in his limp hand is warm; he gulps what's left.

"Hello," she says. "Joe?"

"Yeah."

"Oh, Joe, are you really being sent to Vietnam?"

There is pressure in the veins of his eyes, and he doesn't speak.

"Joe?" she says.

"Looks that way."

"Oh, Joe, how awful."

"Yeah."

"How did it happen?"

"I just came down on orders, is all."

"What does that mean?"

"Well, it's kind of hard to explain."

"Where are you, Joe? Are you in a bar?"

"Sure am; sure as hell am."

"Are you having a good time? How do you feel?"

"Not bad."

"How's everything else been going, all right?"

"What do you mean?"

"You know. How are you otherwise?"

"Okay, I guess. Sure."

"Would you like to come over, have a drink with Bob and me?"

"Would that be all right?"

"Of course it would, if you'd like to do it."

"I would, yes, honest. I mean, if it's all right with you. I'm fine. It doesn't even matter to me, I've got so much other stuff to worry about, you know what I mean, Sharon?"

"Well, come on over then. It's the least we can do."

"I mean, I don't care that you're married, that's what I mean."

"I know."

"I'll come by cab, all right?"

"Could we come and get you?"

"No, no, cab's all right."

"All right. See you in a little."

Eagerness is in her voice, one quick flare of it. She savors her words, loving to say them, glad, it occurs to him suddenly, that she is married and he has called out of need because he has no friend but her in the city.

"Are you hungry?" she says. "I'll throw on a steak if you are."

"All right."

"And hurry, Joe. I want to hear all about what you're doing. I'm so glad you called."

There was an afternoon one Sunday, when rain and nearing storms made the air gray, and they sat in the living room, drinking with Sharon's sister, Caroline, and Caroline's fiancé, Fred, and Sharon dared Fred, who was a shade older, making him feel that there was a bet in the air between them and he could win and have her if he wanted. Though she was to be a sister-in-law in his future, she could not find the will or the means or the reason to restrain herself. That was her message: caprice was her queen.

Sitting at the bar to have one last beer before leaving, Whitaker watches the bartender, a vigorous, healthy-looking man upon whose left hand the absence of three fingers causes in Whitaker a small but exacting shock. He can think no more. He wants to call the man "club fingers," and wave farewell with his fist.

Bob and Sharon greet him at the door. Sharon kisses him twice. Bob shakes his hand. Bob is thin; his hair is black.

"It's so good to see you, Joe."

Bob wears a white shirt and a silky blue tie set in the wide flourish of a perfect Windsor knot. His trousers are neatly creased, his shirt trimly tucked in. He wears a wedding ring and another ring is on the little finger of his left hand. The neatness of his thick hair, blacker than Sharon's, speaks of twice-a-week trimmings.

Standing at the liquor cabinet, he says, "Can I get you something to drink?"

"Sure."

Sharon wears the pink skirt of a suit that Whitaker remembers because it shows netted stockings and hints of skin well into the slope of her thigh. The white blouse is speckled with pink and the frills at the throat are pink also. She wears no shoes and sits curled up on her legs, like a cat, in a cuplike leather chair.

"Whiskey all right?"

"Fine," Whitaker says.

"Little water?"

"No. Just ice."

"So, tell us everything you've been doing, Joe."

"I've been drinking. Since early this afternoon, mostly I've been drinking."

"Drowning your sorrows," Sharon says, expectancy the light and smile of her eye.

"Looking for a good time?" Bob says.

"I don't know. I was over by the Washington Monument."

"Right, right," Sharon nods.

"I just wandered around."

"Observed," Bob says.

"I didn't really participate."

"I see."

"How's everything between you two?"

"Fine, Joe. Just fine," she says, just the smallest huskiness entering her voice, a depth and echo in which her love of sex, along with her skill at it, are the real wonders of which she is speaking—would he care to try?

"How exactly did you meet Sharon, Joe?" Bob says.

"I picked her up on a train."

"Now that's not really true," she says.

"It's nearly true."

"We met on a train and talked."

"How did you meet Sharon, Bob?"

"Same high school."

He ached to lie within her, to move into and out of her body and make her feel him fiercely, and know of him so that she, in her thighs, her cunt, would remember.

"We grew up about six blocks from each other," Bob says.

"How is it that you have to go to Vietnam, Joe?" she says.

"Came down on orders."

"I thought they were mostly marines over there," Bob says.

"What does that mean? 'Came down on orders.'"

"Somebody at the Pentagon and this IBM computer got together and came up with my name, so they sent the word on down to Fort Meade to get me and they got me."

"Who does that work?"

"Other soldiers."

"There are civilians who do it, too, aren't there?" Bob says.

"I guess so," says Whitaker and stands up.

"Sure," Bob says.

Crossing between them to the liquor cabinet where he detects a scent of mint, Whitaker feels the disapproval of their eyes upon him, but he is a ghost in their house, a ghost in the world now, so what can they, with their praise or their condemnation, matter? With golden tongs he reaches into a golden bucket and picks two cubes of ice, which he drops into a clean glass. The bourbon he pours over them changes their color. He begins to talk about Parnelli Jones and A. J. Foyt, auto racing, the power of machines, the majesty of cars and how they were like dogs, pets, good beasts, but you had to be stronger, better, in control. And the day Parnelli won his first big race, Al Keller, a veteran of twenty-three years, got killed, flipping into a chain-link barrier and landing atop the retaining wall.

To speak her good night to him, Sharon strolls over to where he is stretched out on the couch, all tucked in with sheets and a blue blanket—they invited him to stay the night when it appeared he would never leave—and her hand settles lightly on his stomach as she speaks, while Bob awaits her, the shape and shadow of him blocking the doorway that leads to the stairs and their bedroom, while Whitaker, just below her lazy, warm fingers, is swollen and hard. Her head is lovely above him, centered in the black luster of her hair, he is so drunk, so very drunk, her eyes so large, sadly appealing, distress in them, and longing beneath the distress, and love of him even further. He is sure she regrets her marriage.

Then she is gone.

Yet for a time he struggles to resist the downward pull of his body drugged with dulling alcohol and exhaustion, for her eyes have put into him the thought that it is not impossible that she might, even here and now, slip down to him to hold him in the later darkness. Though immediately before him the streetlight above the glowing park is visible in the window, like a picture in a frame. He remembers the newspaper they shared not so long ago, the remnants moving with wind among the trees that hid him from her earlier this afternoon. He wants her to want him. Night and day. Wrong or right. His feelings swoop around, murky and sad. I'm going out of my head, he thinks, and then he recognizes that his thoughts are song lyrics. What do cars say to one another? he thinks. They putt and sputter. What in the person is the spark?

9

Buried beneath blankets, he is startled by consciousness, as if at the entrance of a calling voice into his slow brain, and then he scarcely moves, listening for over an hour to the silence of their house. Pain thumps in his skull. The clock on the wall shows it is nearly six A.M. He stands slowly, tentatively, alert to the possibility of nausea coming strong enough to send him flopping back onto the couch. He waits for a while. The sickness in him, however, is not severe. Uncomfortable, but not incapacitating. He does not know how long they stayed together, drinking. No certain knowledge informs him of the evening's end.

Pulling on his trousers, he puts on his shirt and shoes. A feeble glow cast by streetlights suffuses the ceiling. The plaster appears to be warped. After prying his shoes back off, he goes carefully to the stairway, which he climbs, leaning heavily upon the banister to make his footsteps lighter. His need to pee is so potent it hurts and he dreams of aspirins, bromo seltzer. The banister, smooth beneath his fingers, lifts him higher. The carpeting cushions his feet. The door to their bedroom is partially open. He opens it farther and is staring in upon the tangle of their bodies. Her breasts are visible, catching light, thick swells of flesh, seeming nearly separate from her, for she is mostly shadow, her hair undone and strewn about her throat, face, and shoulder. Her mouth is open, breathing. The first time he got her was on the floor, afraid to move to the bed because the lapse of time might have cost his rhythm, her desire and willingness. He kept her hot with one hand, getting the rubber on with the other. What a lie he's telling; he's never had her. She had him, though. He wasn't fast enough with the rubber and she squirmed away. She told him to stop and he did. Then she told him to start, and he did. She was way out front, looking back, watching him hope that he was somebody. But she knew better. And then she kept inviting him back. But just to sit there. Just to hear, "Stop."

After peeing he returns to the bedroom doorway. Now her breathing changes. He looks. Pink lips encircle the dark socket of her mouth. They screwed last night, Bob and her. Whitaker is sure, hurting as he thinks of it. That was the meaning of their evening, though Whitaker tried to take it from them. They joined together with Whitaker between them, and their joining killed him. If she had desired Whitaker even for a minute, Bob rode in on that desire. He senses now their tactic, the struggle between them. They fed this day of their life with the food of ole Whitaker. He feels he can smell the sweat of their meeting, coupling, for if she were ever to make this man, her husband, believe in her dream of herself as a creature of the wilds tempted by flight, then her disappearance must seem, at times, a danger. On this day, Whitaker helped her prove it was truly possible that she might, on a whim, or no basis at all, run away from her home and husband, so Bob nailed her, seized her flesh where she would most feel his presence and nailed her, held her upon the power of his will and prick until she wished for nothing more than sleep, happy that he panicked so exquisitely and completely at her smallest intimation of their danger, her threat of a threat.

But what of me? thinks Whitaker.

Trousers, a shirt, a tie, and socks are arranged upon a straight-backed chair near the foot of the bed. Softly Whitaker strides across the room. Close enough to hear Bob and Sharon's breathing, which draws his own into their rhythm, he pats Bob's trouser pockets. He rummages for Bob's billfold. Inside are two twenties, five tens, two fives, four ones. He takes a one, a five, two tens, one twenty. From his pocket, he draws out his handkerchief with which he wipes clean the leather before returning it to the trousers. Her perfect body is the body of a perfect toy. He does not want to leave her to this other, and wonders suddenly, glimpsing a steeple out the window, is there anyone out there now at the monument where he was, the monument to Washington, or at the mall or reflecting pool? If he were to go there now, would he be the only marcher or would there be others sickened with some protest, some soundless howling? Thinking this, the words melting and slowly transferring into emotion, he feels he has joined in a movement with thousands and thousands of other people.

Outside, he sits awhile in the park.

10

Of the two movies, Lan found the second more pleasing and intriguing, a story named after the event of people going into a forest with food and drink, everybody sharing everything in a party. In the story the people who are old tried to change the young girl into someone as old as they were. Then a boy who was nearly a giant, and very beautiful, came among them. There was lovely dancing amid colored lights and paper decorations on a barge in a river shining like the wet sides of a fish, the girl and boy dancing, she in her thin blue dress, filmy as air, and he with his shirtsleeves rolled up to the elbows. They loved each other, truly. In the end, he ran from her through weeds as high as his waist, pursuing a big train pulling many boxes of different colors, while the young girl among the old people waited until she could no longer, and she ran to find him.

Now Lan is standing beside the Lambretta driver who brought her home. They linger before the narrow alleyway that leads to the tiny hut in which she lives. Having ridden with Kim out of Bien Hoa as far as Tan Mai, she walked with Kim to her home. Kim's mother offered tea, and asked about the movies. Lan sat for a while, then waved down the scooter that took her to the highway and off and down a dirt road of ruts to the village of An Duc To. The driver, having been paid, sits astride his scooter, chatting for a moment before smiling and stepping to the ground to turn his vehicle about.

Streaking suddenly up from the fields to their left, the flare startles them, hissing, shedding sparks; then it pops and hangs in silence above the weeds, the logs, a pulse of drifting light over the flat, wavering land that leads to the jungle facing the bunker. They stand transfixed until the machine gun in the bunker begins to chatter; the muzzle flashes, pauses, then shakes again; the bursts are short, repetitive; the tracer rounds flee like greenish sticks of fire down the dark. Lan, having ducked to take the thin protection of a tree, has a moment's vision of the men behind that weapon peering into a wilderness of rustling, threatening forms. The silence goes on. The flare, beneath its shadow of silk, lessens. The dark thickens. The speed of the flare's descent doubles. As it nears the ground, the lines that hold it aloft are threads of light. With wind, it sways. The gun, having received no fire in response, is silent. The flare, sputtering, goes out.

"Nothing," he says.

"No. It happens all the time and they always shoot"—she gestures to indicate the inky wall of foliage—"that way. No one ever shoots back."

"Good," he says, and grins. "You should be happy."

"Oh, yes." Lan smiles. "But I don't know why they do it."

"They think the trees move."

"What?"

"They lay out there all night, they think the trees move. They shoot at the trees. They get bored, they shoot at trees." He is elderly, his face like leather, with a wisp of beard and white eyebrows as thick as silkworms. He shakes his head, smiling, before nodding good night and driving off. The red speck of the taillight of his machine dissolves slowly in the dark. For a moment more she watches, and then, feeling tired, humming quietly, she turns into the alleyway.

They are waiting for her, the two GIs. She sees them and halts in the shadows before they know she is there. Each holding a bottle of *Ba Moi Ba* beer, they rest against her neighbor's wall, while Pham Van Doan, a Lambretta driver she does not like and who she is certain brought them, squats near a jeep that must be theirs. His elbows are on his knees, his hands under his chin. Moonlight touches them all. Here, beyond the first of the little streets, stand numerous homes with figures visible all about the yards—people sitting, resting, sharing conversation. Le Xuan Thuc, a farmer from near Dong Xoai who lost his land and family in the fighting there, is some twenty yards away at work before a lantern. An old man of great seriousness, he lives now with his sister and carves, with extreme concern and caution, figurines of animals in wood. At a juncture in the pathways, an open welding shop shows young men laboring within a clanging celebration of sparks; they are bright with sweat, hammers swinging in their hands.

She steps from her concealment and the three men stir in recognition of her arrival. Pham Van Doan hastens to inform her that he brought the GIs, How much will she pay him for helping her business? Fifty, she says, knowing the GIs will have already paid him something. He yells in protest, demanding more. "Too little, too little." She shuts her eyes, but does not tell him that he annoys her, that she is tired, that she does not like him. She puts the money in his hand and he dumps it to the ground. She shrugs and goes on. She hears him call her a slut, a vile perfume, a dead flower. Without looking back, she senses him bend to the money, then run off to wherever he left his taxi.

One of the two GIs is a black man of slight build; the other is larger and white and both are dressed in their work clothes, the green uniforms that bear their names and insignias. The larger, the white, winking, gestures a greeting.

She nods. "Hello, GI," she says. "Hello, pretty. You come see Lan, huh?"

"That's right, Girl. You got it; me and Sissler here."

She studies the other one, the black one, concentrating on his nametag and thinking about what she just heard. "Okay, Sissler."

"The two of us," Sissler says; his eyes are large. He rubs his fingers on the bumps and stubble of his chin. "Ryan, I got to say she don't look like a lotta fun."

"Fun. Sure," she says. "You want short-time, Lan, huh?"

"I tole you," Ryan says. "I tole you I was bringin' you to the right place. Man, I know my way."

"You can do short-time?" Sissler says.

"No sweat."

"Two men. Two men."

"Okay. I know."

"Do short-time one man, fini him, do short-time second man," he says, raising his first and second fingers to show her. "Two men."

"I know," she says, grinning. "I 'stand."

"Whatcha say?"

"Can do. Can do number one. I show you. House me."

"How much?" Sissler says.

"House me," she tells them. "C'mon." With a small copper key, she pops open the flimsy lock on the door of corrugated tin nailed to a rough wood frame. Shadows, as they enter, wash over her. She closes and hooks shut the door.

"Palatial," Sissler says. "Really number one."

"What time is it?"

"What?"

"What time is it?" Ryan says.

"I can't see my watch. But we got time."

"Let's goooo, girl." He is singing the words.

"Okay," Lan says. She is bowed over, rummaging about in a chest in the corner.

"This place's the pits, man," Sissler says. "We in the bottom of the barrel."

Ryan halfway sings, " 'Love is not a gadget, love is not a toy.' "

From the chest in the corner, she returns with a lantern along with a match, the head of which, pressed and scraped beneath the cardboard cover, puffs into fire. Tipped to the lantern wick, it touches the room with a trembling yellow. She smiles, walking proudly before them. "Number one, huh?"

"GE," Ryan says. "How much?" He puffs on a cigarette while Sissler paces the perimeter of the room.

"Tomorrow house me more good," she tells them. "I fini house tonight."

"I know that," Sissler says. "I know that. How much?"

"Short-time? Two men, seven hundred okay?" She smiles, nodding.

"Get outta here," Ryan yells. "Four hundred."

"Oh, no can do. *Xin loi.* No can do four hundred."

Ryan springs at her and his hands take her waist between them, making her cry aloud. "No hurt me," she says, "no hurt me," as he flings her upward and holds her poised above his grinning face cut with shadow. "Four hundred," he tells her. "Okay?"

"Okay."

"I mean, we really don't have to give you nothin', do we, slope? Do we?"

"I don't know."

"No. We don't, because you're a stupid goddamn whore. Ain't that what you are? Why don't you answer me? We ain't leavin' here without gettin' some anyway, so why all the sweat? Don't you know that?"

"No sweat."

"You make me sick, all the sweat you put a man through."

"No sweat, GI. Fini hold me, okay? No hold me."

"How much?" he says.

"What you want—I don't know."

"Three hundred."

"I no like hold me, hurt me."

"Three hundred. Just remember we come all the way over here to help you in this shitty-assed country."

"You fini!"

"Two men. Three hundred."

"No sweat."

"For how many times?"

"Okay, okay."

"For how many times?"

"I no 'stand!"

"One, two, three, four—each man, how many?"

"I don't know."

He embraces her, squeezing hard. "That's good," he says. "You got it. Now just drop your drawers; we think we love you."

"We pretty sure."

She nods; her throat hurts, and on the bed behind her, Sissler sits undressing in the changing light as Ryan crosses before the lantern.

"I don't know why you do me bad, GI, I don't know." She is pulling off the tops of her pajamas before carefully folding them. Sissler, behind her, is unhooking the catch of her bra.

"Sissler," Ryan says.

"Yeah."

"That Sergeant Koopman don't get off my case, I am going to do something insane."

"You got to ignore the fuckhead."

"You see how he treats me."

"You got to pay him no mind."

"You see how he hassles me."

"Yeah." He hands Lan the bra. "But you got to ignore him."

After placing the bra at the foot of the bed, she returns to him to sit slantwise across his knees.

"I got to get back to the world is what I got to do."

"We here now," Sissler says.

"Why him do me bad, Sissler?" Her gaze is genuine upon him; she wants to know.

"'Cause he's crazy," Sissler says. "'Cause he's crazy ofay Georgia trash and that's why."

Ryan laughs loudly; he stomps his feet, waves his arms.

"You laugh; do me bad, I no like. You come, talk me short-time, I say, 'Okay, no sweat.' Why do me bad?" And with

Sissler so near, she turns to him for an answer, and that makes him put his mouth to her throat. "One man all night, GI. You, okay?" Sissler smiles; she feels the smile against her throat. "No sweat; no money," she says. "You want all night? Fini two men, then one man all night. Sleep all night, GI." He smiles again, looking at her, a peculiar smile, mostly in his eyes, barely altering his expression.

"Sure," he says.

"Can do, huh?" She is nodding eagerly. His hands are on her buttocks, moving; his fingers tug at the elastic of the waist of the pajamas. "No . . . sweat," she says while touching one finger gently to his temple.

"See you later, Ryan," he says.

"I got your smokes, Sis. I'm gonna wait outside."

"I fini clothes . . . no sweat," she whispers and hastens to get out of the pajama bottoms, before lying back on the matting of woven straw over planks in the uneasy gleam of the lantern, her thighs parting to calm him, it takes no effort, she knows what it all is, and when he is replaced by Ryan, her only sense of the difference is weight, a greater heaviness, a heavier rhythm, as she lies unmoving in the ice of her thoughts. Then a gecko high in the rafters unleashes a moment of its eerie chatter and misery startles her, one long knife of it that snakes her arms around him who is over her, Ryan, white, thick, angry Ryan so close to her now, and she is stammering and crying aloud. He falters, surprised at her frenzy, and then he watches whatever is happening to her happen, grinning and looking and calling out, "I think I made her come," to Sissler, who calls back through the thin metal wall, "Just hurry up."

11

Her eyes are ancient; they are strange and exact as olives. She is alone. The GIs are gone; they have been gone for some time, and she doesn't know for how long, nor does she know of the place to which they have gone; they appeared and disappeared; it could have mattered. Recollection of her agitated voice asking the one to stay puzzles and insults her. Now she's glad both are gone. Maybe she was frightened of the one and sought protection from the other. She feels cramped and thick in her middle, in her stomach and back, a faint ache on the right side; she will bleed soon; perhaps tomorrow; if not tomorrow, then the next day; the bleeding will keep her from work.

And suddenly she blinks, jolted by the memory of her dead father's hands. The thought has come for no reason. The air has eyes, it seems, generations of her curious ancestors. It makes her lie in perfect stillness for a time. In three days it will be the day she goes to Saigon to see her brother and give him money. Maybe she can also buy a new dress. Her brother needs the money to pay for certain papers without which he would be immediately taken into the army. Some time ago, after serving six months, he was given a temporary release because of consumption. The papers he paid for said the illness remained in him. He doesn't know if it does or if it doesn't. Still, she lies unmoving and naked in a continuing silence, her clothing tossed wherever they threw it. Bugs of varied shells and instincts bat about the lantern, the queer configurations of their bodies magnified in shadow on the walls. One glides to her knee, and prowls a moment before settling upon a cut in the skin. With feathery extensions jutting from its shoulders, it probes the wound. She swallows, her cheeks growing large with breathing, while the tentacles seek the openness of the sore, and her eyes, in weariness, close. Then slowly, with care and determination, she forces herself to stand, fit her feet into slippers, and walk to the chest in the corner. Opening the lid, she draws forth a robe of purple silk patterned with large and delicate flowers. After covering herself and tying the belt of the robe at her waist, she locates a metal box bound by cord, and taking up from the bed the 300 piastres the GIs left and the 550 Madame Lieu paid her, she deposits it all in the box with her paper money, red and green, a mix of silverish and copper-colored coins. She secures the cord, returns the box to the chest, and covers it with a square of folded silk. There is a book, *The Tale of Kieu,* with ink-drawn figures of Kieu and Kim faintly occupying the cover. Under it lies a *Playboy* magazine that she took from Madame Lieu's, the glossy pages bent open to reveal Miss August. She places them both on top of the silk, then closes and locks the lid of the chest. She picks the two prophylactics from the floor and drops them into a paper sack, which she places beside the door. And there, crouched in the corner gloom, waits a rat the size of a small child. She goes rigid; the eyes are bright and interested, looking at her with an unnatural glint. And then something happens; it happens deep in the brain behind the eyes of that rat and she sees it: the animal knows her.

With a basin and towel snatched up from a table near the bed, she goes sideways into the night in which the sky is cloudless. There is an icy edge to the air and Le Xuan Thuc remains at his workbench in the small yard before his house, having endured even into this late hour. It stops her to see him. The tiny body of a tiger rests in his hands; the liquid he uses on his knife as he works shimmers in a jar at his feet. He seems worried and somber, quietly working. His hands are exacting, his breathing a secretive whisper. The eyes in the head of the tiger are as smooth as bulbs of glass. Possessed of precision and detail, they are set in rims of fine sockets. He dips the blade of the knife in the jar. Carefully, he puts the point to the paw. For a moment she watches, waiting till the knife is safely withdrawn from its task before she says softly, "Good evening," to him and when he looks up in acknowledgment, she explains that she was going out to wash. He returns to his work. She wonders if she might stay to watch his hands performing movements so intricate, but then turns to go. She is tired; she will wash and sleep. She walks swiftly, traveling through swaths of moonlight and shadow until she arrives at a tree and the well. From a low branch she hangs the towel, and bending, sets the pan on a flatness of rock. Unfastening the bucket of wood from its hook, she lowers it into the ringing depths and for the length of one moment gazes into the loveliness of the walls spiraling down to the bucket swaying and the blackness shimmering. Then the rope runs from her fingers. The splash seems in another world. The well changes into a dark hole falling away beneath her. Hand over hand she hauls up her burden of water. With soap she lathers and washes, and with the towel carefully dries. She is thinking, and it seems new knowledge has come to her in her day. If you moved when they were in you, they liked it better; if you moved and made sounds with your breathing. How strange Heaven is, she thinks, recalling Madame Lieu's car wash and the other girls there, her companions in misery. *The Tale of Kieu* is right. Heaven gives them rosy-cheeked youth and beauty, but then He banishes them to the windblown dust of the world, where they must live in dishonor before gaining His mercy. As she dresses under the watchful black sky, she feels the truth of the great poem written long ago, but born, it seems, of her life. Several wary paces into the forest, she empties the water onto the leaves and brittleness of a branch.

Le Xuan Thuc is packing up his tools. He moves slowly, wearily, as she approaches. She is close to her door when he says, "You should not bring the soldiers here. Why do you do it?"

"I did not bring them. It was Pham Van Doan."

The old man considers something that weighs heavily upon him and only gradually can other thoughts push it away. "Like the eel you burrow in the mud, Lan, and yet you give money to your family, so in that you are a good daughter."

Within her house, she shuts the door tightly, then fixes the hook. She folds the towel. She settles the bucket in the corner. She watches through the window as Thuc hobbles from sight. At the chest, she unlocks the lid and withdraws *The Tale of*

Kieu with its faded cover. She lights one candle and sits on the side of the bed. She finds easily the chapter she wants. The candlelight flows over the pages:

> *My daughter, retorted the old Panderess, all men are alike. Do you think they would come here for nothing? In this profession there still exist many other amusing things: games of hide and seek by night, intimacy or gay company by day. Listen to this, my daughter, and keep this in mind: there are seven interior attitudes and eight intimate techniques to amuse people until they are sated with the willow-flower, until you can turn them upside down like stones, and until they completely lose consciousness.*

She can't help it. She begins to imagine Madame Lieu attempting such instructions at the car wash. After some seconds she grows amused, giggling finally. She reads a while more, then closes the book, ready for sleep.

12

While he stands in line, Whitaker counts the heads of the soldiers preceding him to the phone booth. They wait under a streetlamp at the edge of the company street. Weary, his face sore from windburn, a curious sadness draws his mind inward. On the rifle range throughout much of the day, he fired at white targets that sprang from the concealment of bushes, logs, and dirt. He popped away with confidence, taking a good weld, the weight of the weapon firmly controlled by his hand snug on the stock. The targets appeared and vanished under each bullet's impact. From a standing position, even the slightest waver made the distant white specks appear to flutter like bits of paper in the wind. Yet he and the magic fuckin' rifle dropped them all, firing with unorthodox precision as the sights fell across the target and held an accurate line for the smallest instant.

Moving forward when the instructor indicated, he worked his sector of terrain, blowing pretend people away until he was startled by one springing up maybe twenty yards in front of him. Because the sights were set for distance, he aimed low and dirt splashed in a little cloud. He overcompensated, and the target didn't respond, nor did the dirt or air. He rushed and got a splash low right. Panicked now, he squeezed hurriedly with no visible effect. The next shot hit low left, then way to the right. "Move on," the instructor told him. "Forget it." But he cannot. He carries it with him through dinner and to the street where the line has grown long behind him by the time his turn comes.

His father will be in bed, he is sure. As he dials the phone, his father's bed is huge in his mind. Its posts are coated with brass. It stands on worn, broken linoleum at the center of the biggest of the upstairs bedrooms in the rickety old house. Whitaker, having spoken to the operator, is depositing the requested change. His father will be there now, lying motionless with his stained old hands at his sides, palms pressed down, shoulders even, eyes wide and fixed on the ceiling as he waits for sleep. Only his brain will be busy, secretly searching for those hidden thoughts that might help him determine the nature of passing time, the nature of waiting. All other drifting specks of ideas will be seen as distractions that must be ignored. With many quilts and blankets piled one on the other upon him, he will be totally still but for the flitting of his eyes. He holds this frozen pose because he believes he is a hunted creature, and if he can keep his pathetic, desperate presence from being discovered, he will never die. Into this old man's thinking tonight will come the ringing of the phone, Whitaker knows, and the old man, already rigid, will tense with self-absorption while the jangling sound of Whitaker's calling floats from the downstairs hallway through all the corridors of that house.

"Hello?" says Roger, his brother.

"Rog? This is Joe."

"Joe?"

"Yeah."

"Hey, what's up?"

"I just thought I'd check on the ole man; this may be the last chance for me to call."

"Nothin' new, Joe. Everything's the same."

"What's he doing? Is he in bed?"

"It's all just the same, I tell you, Joe."

"He's incredible."

"Man, do I know."

"Could I talk to him, you suppose?"

"He won't come to the phone, Joe."

"Ask him."

"There's no point, Joe. Honest, once he's in bed, he don't budge for nothin'."

"Yeah."

"Once he gets all bundled up, that's it."

"I know."

"He's afraid of the transitions, that's what it comes down to. I been doin' a lot of thinkin' about it. Cold to warm. Warm to cold. Ever since the doctor explained to him all that stuff about his heart and blood and how it works."

"He's scared. That's what I think."

"Takes him half a year to move. I wish you'd called before he got into bed."

"I couldn't, Rog. How could I? You should see the line a guys waitin' behind me now. This is the first chance I had to get to the phone. I had to wait I don't know how long, and all these other guys are still behind me."

"I know it's tough on you, too, Joe. That's all I'm sayin'. Listen, you wanna say hi to Bonnie?"

"Bonnie? You on a date?"

"Yeah. You wanna say hi?"

"Listen, Rog, I didn't interrupt anything, did I?"

"No, no."

"Just tell her hi for me, okay?"

"Mom called the other night."

"No kidding."

"Drunk as a skunk."

"Lucky you."

"You can say that again."

"What'd she have to say for herself?"

"I kid you not. I couldn't understand a word. She said, 'Mmmmgumph,' and you know, gobbledygook."

"I wonder what she wanted."

"Your guess is as good as mine."

"Listen, Rog," he says, "we ought to get an extension phone put into the ole man's room. See how much it'd cost. Check it out and let me know. I'll send you the money."

"You wanna?"

"Yeh."

"Okay."

"Look into it."

"Okay."

"And tell him I called; tell him I'll write soon as we get over there. I'm not gonna call anymore."

"Okay."

"See you in a year."

"Bonnie says bye."

"Bye, Bonnie."

"Right, Joe. Take care."

"You, too."

He steps from the booth and goes past the murmuring line of men under a pale cloud of cigarette smoke. The air has a slight chill. While thinking of his father, his mind is entered by a sky of snowflakes turning, descending, for it is winter and there would be snow in the Midwest. The snowflakes fall as he walks for a time, covering the land, until it occurs to him how much they are like the targets he shot at in that darkening afternoon. He thinks for a while of the one he missed. He cannot penetrate to the cloudy center of his inability to bring hand, rifle, and eye into harmony sufficient to knock that target flat. It nags his mind, and slowly, one very large, targetlike snowflake transforms itself into a man with a yellow face and hands aiming a rifle. "Shit," says Whitaker. "Oh," and he grabs at his stomach. "Oh, oh, he'd a shot me to shit." He gasps and groans, weaves left before right, falling to his knees only to rise in teeth-clenching melodrama and then collapse sideways into the damp grass where he lies grinning and looking at the stars. *I know you don't know what I'm goin' through. But I can tell you that it makes me feel bad. It hurts and I'm so sad.* He rolls onto his stomach. More fucking song lyrics. He chuckles and pushes against the ground to get up. Poor Roger. He can just hear his mom drunk out of her gourd talking gobbledygook. And his poor brother has to pick up the phone.

In the dayroom, where he goes, a few of the members of his unit, some of them brand-new arrivals, people he's never seen before, listlessly watch TV. He sits for a time among them, smoking a cigarette.

13

With men he scarcely knows, Whitaker bunks on the ground floor of a two-story barracks, and as the sun rises on the morning of their departure, he is awake to watch it stain the tree and sky that fill the window across from him. The struts and beams are rough, unsanded, like parts of a barn. At first the dark lines and bulges of the tree are vague against the ink black spaces beyond, in which light seems frail and impossible, appearing, disappearing, fragments and streaks, flashes and ultimately waves that arrive to touch and hold the limbs and show their bark in detail. He does not know how long he has been awake.

"If it's the day I think it is," says a voice, "I am feelin' I got to go on sick call. Got some kind of sickness in me. Bad, too, like TB or typhoid." It's Rowe speaking, a huge, older black Spec

Five who was in Korea with the artillery. "Malaria. Can't go nowhere. Too sick."

"Me, too," says a southern voice. "Ah broke my damn leg in my sleep. Never had such a fall."

"Who's gonna believe that?" says Whitaker. He just wants to say something.

"Not nobody," says Rowe.

"None a you," Whitaker tells them, not really knowing what he's saying.

A whistle screams and screams, getting closer with each blast. It sticks, they know, from the bulbous lips of First Sergeant O'Conner, ordering them to the first formation of the day.

The air is clean and icy cold. They stand in the rectangular, four-lined shape of a platoon, though they are no real platoon, but only a haphazard, hurriedly gathered assortment of strangers. First Sergeant O'Conner paces as they arrange themselves. Some wear gloves. The wind flaps in huge swaths that sweep across them like chilling blows, making their eyes water. First Sergeant O'Conner faces them to announce the schedule. There is much to be done. He spells out their day hour by hour. They will be traveling by commercial jet. Before 2300 hours they will be in San Francisco boarding the troopship USNS *Woodrow Wilson,* moored out there at the edge of the sea.

A school bus goes by, loaded with children.

Breakfast is eggs, bacon or ham, orange or tomato juice, fried potatoes, rolls and butter, milk or coffee or tea. They eat from tan plastic trays that, like the trays of infants, are sectioned into various shapes. Whitaker is surprised by the enormity of his appetite, for he had anticipated a stomach slack and sickened with worry. Like A.J. or Parnelli on the morning of a big race.

After breakfast their duffel bags must be loaded onto a deuce-and-a-half truck, which will then be driven to the Baltimore airport. One of the unit's NCOs suggests that the bags be transported from the barracks to the truck through a human chain, but after some discussion between Captain Bell and First Sergeant O'Conner, it is decided that each man will carry his own gear. In this way responsibility will remain individual. Whitaker is among the last to sling the burden of that bag up into the canvas-hooded truck where sixty or so others are already stacked like the corpses of so many dwarfs together in a cave. Three men follow Whitaker, dragging and hefting their bags before the driver checks the stability of the load and slams the tailgate up into place. Thin as a rake handle, this gray-haired, lifer-loser Pfc whistles as he inserts the hooks that make the gate secure, and circling the truck, he kicks all ten of the massive tires. Finally, held in an expression of deep thought, he stands inert for an instant, scanning again the length and breadth of his task. Clearing his throat, shaking his head, he spins to salute Captain Bell who, though surprised by the move, manages nevertheless to return the gesture with some poise.

"I'll take her in now, sir," the man says.

"You do that, Barlow."

"Yes, sir."

They lie on their bunks in the still air of the overheated barracks for the remainder of the morning. There is the music of many portable radios tuned to various stations and set at low volume, for nearly every soldier owns one. At eleven o'clock, they have police call, because Captain Bell wants every bit of trash cleaned from the area his people occupied. He tells them he wants their area left immaculate. They form a line, arms extended to create the proper spacing in daylight heated now by the higher, fuller sun. Paper, tin, gum wrappers, cigar and cigarette butts, everything but the grass itself is to be picked up. That is their order. Rasputin, a coffee-colored black from Watts, carries his huge plastic transistor radio; the dials are white; a blue grill covers the speaker. He strolls to the music and refuses to pick up anything from the ground. "What they gonna do to me? I don't pick up this shit," he says. "What they gonna do, send me to Vietnam?" He shakes his head; he strolls and laughs.

Whitaker agrees, but keeps on bending, obeying. Sprinkled all through the grass, he sees innumerable cinders whose presence he cannot explain.

The noon meal is meat loaf with lumps of tomato, a sauce and chips of onion, carrots, peas, baked potatoes, apple pie or ice cream, coffee, milk or tea. The evening meal, they are told, will be aboard the plane.

At four fifteen they are called into formation wearing fatigues and field jackets, pistol belts, baseball caps, and black gloves. They carry AWOL bags containing toothbrushes, toothpaste, shaving gear, all other personal items. Slung on their shoulders are their M14 rifles, and they stand in the wintry dusk for nearly an hour while the barracks doors are locked, checked, double checked, the guards and CQ relieved of duty. By bus they go out of Fort Meade onto the highway and along the highway until they come to the Baltimore airport, where they drive past the terminal to a waiting civilian in a tie and sports coat who climbs aboard to guide them through a gate marked NO ADMITTANCE and onto the immense emptiness, the desolation, of the tarmac. One hour later, they are marched across the concrete in a column of twos. The plane before them appears tarnished and dull, the color of a spoon. No stewardess attends them and they are seated in the rear section.

At Kansas City where there is a layover, they are allowed to stroll around outside the plane for thirty minutes of their two-hour delay, but they are forbidden to enter the terminal. After takeoff, the pressure that builds up in the ears of one of the men does not release. He pounds his head and groans and starts to cry.

On the ground in San Francisco, they are marched through the mammoth terminal with their weapons on their shoulders, a phenomenon that people notice and smile at. A child imitates their marching. Then a waiting army captain shows the way to the luggage point where they pick up their duffel bags. A bus, glowing at the curb, opens its doors and they are driven down some highways, through some countryside, past residential and factory areas and into the sudden spectacle of acres of concrete and a gathering mass of other buses.

The ship is an immense black wall the length of a city block at the base of which they are deposited and formed into a single-file line. MPs in white helmets and gloves will check them aboard. Someone near Whitaker whispers that San Francisco is across the bay. Empty trucks, coils of wire, surround them. From his place near the tail of the line, Whitaker peers forward to the milky white helmets of the MPs who stand at the gangplank upon which he will step and walk to the hole of the hatchway. He puts down the burden of his duffle bag. The butt of his rifle, moving as he moves, bumps against his thigh. He has been passed from hand to hand—picked up, shifted, abandoned, set down, delivered by a hundred thousand cooperating hands. He imagines giants, and himself as tiny as a toy in enormous palms and fingers. The ship before him seems no vessel of adventure but rather a wall through which he cannot see San Francisco. Hello, he thinks, hello. City of a thousand faces, city of the Golden Gate, where little cable cars go . . . here and . . . there . . .

He stops suddenly, blinking, as if the final hand, huge and icy pale, has dropped him, so he stands there.

14

Now he can no longer even glimpse the land that a moment ago lay like a shadow cast down upon the flat and comprehensive sea. They left Cam Ranh Bay in the late afternoon, having arrived in the night, hovering midchannel for fifteen hours, like exiles, while cargo and other units were transferred to shore. Jungle was visible beyond the sandy beaches, the wood and tin of the Quonset huts and other buildings. When first sighted, the land had seemed a great black rock, crusted and rigid amid ceaseless waves. Jungle was all they'd heard about. That Vietnam should seem a scorched black rock was a surprise.

Now Whitaker is alone, remembering, wondering. At departure there was a dim scarlet above the shore of stone and green vegetation. The falling sun coated the jungle in a wet-seeming lushness, and a man from another unit began to talk to Whitaker about how he wished he'd brought packets of seeds. He'd like to have a garden. Especially tomatoes. But then he worried that he'd probably have to guard his garden. Pull guard on his garden. "No more flying fish," he observed. He was right. The schools of flying fish that had accompanied them like pets in the open sea, leaping and staying above the chopped-up blue, were nowhere to be seen. "They must be scared, too," the man said. They passed scattered ships and silver seaplanes, moored and bobbing. They sailed from the harbor and curved south toward Saigon and into evening.

Now the moon, round and ragged like a carelessly packed snowball, slides through gray and gray-black mists. The glow off the air and water is the glow from off new snow when Whitaker was a kid. He is in a silver sea headed into a horizon he cannot find. Beyond the bow, the line of the horizon, sweeping in from the right and left, dissolves into smokiness, a dim, glowing haze. The tall rocking spire of their mast with its small constant light rises into a sky so precisely black it feels ghostly. Earlier, when he wandered to the fantail, he strolled among resting troopers and one enchanted sailor staring up into what was then a delicate blue shimmer. Whitaker stands pressed against a slanted, chest-level rail of riveted metal plates. High to his left hangs a lifeboat covered in canvas. Someone begins to play the harmonica. The notes fall one after the other. They cannot shape themselves into music. Whitaker thinks about how he has always meant to learn to play a musical instrument. Perhaps the harmonica, or the guitar. Carefully, thoughtfully, he fits his hands to the rail and leans forward until he is looking down the steep hull to where the ocean thrashes of its own will, it seems to him, because it wants to, rather than in response to the cumbersome advance of the ship. Swells and crests roll up white, slide high, then level; they contain exact diamonds. Areas of snowlike foam appear and then dissolve and there is a constant rushing, washing sound, the dull and distant rasp and thud of the engine.

A figure passes behind him; he straightens; it is one of the merchant marines who run the ship. An older, fuzzy-faced man, his weather-beaten skin is as wrinkled as his clothing, which appears to have been slept in. Whitaker spent much of the afternoon arguing with a pimple-faced merchant marine about who would win if a fight broke out between the soldiers and the merchant marines. They knew the ship, could hide, ambush, the merchant marine said. They could cut the power. The soldiers had flashlights, Whitaker told him, and were trained to fight. The merchant marines had all kinds of weapons stashed away, knives, crossbows. This older man says nothing, floating in the half-light and dropping down a staircase with no sound other than the whisper of his hands on the rail, putting into Whitaker's mind his father, a poor old ruin of a farmer who never lived in any city. A dark old stalwart stained with tobacco juice, wind, and sun, his life formed him beyond any chance of change until he was felled two years ago by a heart attack that hit like a sledgehammer crashing into the brain of a steer in the slaughterhouse.

It knocked him flat and gasping. His breath shouted inside his swelling neck. To learn that the fine, pumping muscle of his heart could grow defective confounded him. The stubborn, reliable muscle of his willpower crumbled, leaving him outraged and a little lost in the wide, wintry land he had trod through and tilled all his life, like a homeward-bound sailor who finds himself upon an unknown sea. Whitaker, staring down the gunmetal gray of the side of the ship, grieves for his lost father. Though Whitaker is on his way to war, at least he is not old.

"Hello, Whitaker," says Rasputin. "Can I talk to you a little?"

"I'm lookin' at the ocean, Rasputin."

"That okay. I just be here talkin' to myself, maybe you can listen, maybe you can't." Rasputin nods, sagely, then glances skyward.

"How can't I if you're standin' right next to me?"

"People do that all the time, man, don't you know that? Yeah, that's the thing I'd like to do, I think, when I get outta this fuckin' army. Study about people thinkin' and the funny shit they do, all that psychological stuff, so I can talk shit to people and fuck up their minds, man, fuck 'em up good. I know that shit and they don't, how they gonna know what I am sayin'? And I can learn all kinds a big words so I can talk shit to people, they just stand there noddin', lookin' real puzzled. Yeah, Whitaker, it all come back to reality, and that's an easy word to say, but a motherfucker to understand." As if struck by a hand no one sees, he stops; his eyes squint, then widen. "Oh," he cries with delight. "Did you hear that? Oh, Mr. Whitaker, did you hear the shit your man was sayin'? 'It all come back to reality, and that an easy word to say, but a mother to understand.' Ain't that some shit. You better get outta here, Whitaker, you get all fucked up in the head bad, you stand around listenin' to me."

Confused as to whether or not Rasputin is mocking him, Whitaker says, "Don't you ever take anything serious, Rasputin? I don't know what you're talking about."

"Sure you do."

"We're on our way to a war, Rasputin."

"That's right. We on a journey. Life is a journey."

"Good night."

"See you soon then."

"I think so."

The night before they docked in Cam Ranh Bay, Captain Bell gathered them to explain that he didn't know whether or not they'd be leaving the ship in the morning, but all troops needed to be prepared to disembark on fifteen minutes' notice. They had to be ready, even though he was pretty sure they would be staying aboard; he was pretty sure their destination was somewhere nearer Saigon and the Bien Hoa area. They would probably get off at the mouth of the Saigon River and proceed by LCM or truck or fixed-wing plane—he didn't know how—to their destination—he didn't know where.

And now they were on their way. Dozing but uneasy, Whitaker wakes up. Rasputin is climbing into his bunk, stacked directly across the narrow aisle. Kenkel, who sleeps above Whitaker, lurches, his stocky body changing the dents in the canvas of his bunk, as he dreams, barely a foot from Whitaker's nose. They are piled on top of one another like bodies on stretchers. Rasputin lies back. His green boxer shorts and T-shirt highlight his dark legs and tufted hair. He arranges his hissing, buzzing radio on his belly and fiddles with the dials for a long time before looking over to Whitaker and nodding. "We way down in the water, Whitaker. No sounds, man."

"You can listen to the fish," says Whitaker.

"Dig it."

15

~~~~~~

Lan presses her hand against the corrugated tin wall while frowning. Her life is so difficult. Anger mixes with sadness, an abrasiveness that rubs the bottom of her brain. They are stealing from her. At work and in her sleep at home. Babysan and ghosts. She wonders if she dare go near the water. Are there water ghosts seeking to infect her with the desire to drown, sneaking and whispering to infect her with the desire to press her face down in water? It is cruel of them, knowing as they do the horror of drowning. Unable to rest because their sunken, irretrievable bodies rot without burial, they are seen sometimes to hover as black clouds above the well or river or pond that took them, murmuring, "It's cold, so cold. . . ." In her home this morning, she awoke with a shock that had her sitting up, a cry bubbling from her lips before she even knew who she was—Quach Ngoc Lan in An Duc To—rising out of sleep in fear of a bad dream of drowning. Goddamn people kicking in her door. They knew her name. She yelled she was somebody else and the person they wanted was not home. They said they didn't care, calling her by name, breaking the door. Callused hands seized her, closed her eyes, and dropped her into water in which she sank, believing desperately that if she did not open her mouth to scream or in any way release the air possessed within her, it would sustain her no matter how deep she sank. Lips compressed, an aching pressure growing within, she went down and down through darkening rings and into, finally, a panic of real suffocation. It sprang her awake, hoping to scream.

And now at work in Tan Mai, she has found a small amount of money gone from her purse. Finishing a thin, blond GI, and wanting to purchase a snack from an approaching peddler, she went to her purse and found forty piastres missing. Babysan, she thinks, glaring, looking about, remembering how those who died in water could have no rest until they drew another victim to their grave to replace them. She wonders, Is the water hungry or lonely that it needs the bodies of people? Is the spirit of drowning in her head? And what of her money? She sees it floating down a well and she falls after it.

Children are always standing about in the shanties. She frowns at the nearest dirt-scabbed urchin; he wears a ragged brown shirt and shorts. Her hatred, though it blazes from her, affects not even the air. She wants to feel his stupid filthy little face break under her punch.

"You numba fuckin' ten," she tells him.

"I can run," he says. "I can run."

"Stupid."

"What do you want, Lan?"

"Get outta here."

"I go, I come back." He shrugs.

"You steal my money."

"No."

"Somebody numba fuckin' ten steal my money."

"I don't know."

"Bulls'it."

"Shine GIs' shoes. Get money. Maybe you don't know your money."

"I know my money. You buy me beer."

A jeep veers into the yard, the dust of its wake continuing to billow and drift down the road, while the driver, an American in colorful civilian clothes, leaps to the ground and trots into the shanty.

"You wanta beer," calls the babysan. "You wanta shine?"

However, the expression on the GI's reddish face is serious and pained; he brushes past the boy, his eyes seeking and holding Lan. "Hello," he says. *Chao co,* Lan.

She smiles, her head buzzing in an effort to identify this face and voice, to find a name, for she can sense the powerful feelings of fondness and familiarity he has for her. They come slanting from his eyes, across the air, to hit a blankness in her. She doesn't know him. "Hello," she says. "Hello, you-you." She hates it when they arrive in civilian clothes, because the uniforms all have their names printed neatly on them, and so many of them believe their presence greatly matters to her; it is good, she knows, to call them by their names. She tries, but there is nothing she can see of him in her past.

"Lan," he is saying, "Lan, Lan," touching her cheek, bowing until his face is close to hers and she feels a little of the kind of intimacy he wants between them. "Listen," he is saying, "no . . . can do . . . same-same fuck-fuck today. Maybe never again. I don't know. You 'stand? You listen. Must go my home America. Tonight. This night. Go airplane. Mamasan me, boucoup sick. Boucoup sick. Mamasan me—she numba one. You 'stand? Maybe die. Maybe fini. Army talk me I can go my home America, talk my mamasan, no die, no fini." In his sadness, his face is flushed and strained; his grief comes off him like heat: "Maybe come back Vietnam," he says. "Maybe yes, maybe no. Army very crazy. Maybe talk me never come back Vietnam; I never see you. I come today talk you good-bye. Lan numba one."

"You go America."

"Yes. So sorry."

"C'mon. Have Coke."

"No."

"Beer."

"No." This second denial has more volume and the swing of the head is wider. He mystifies her with his sadness, for now his eyes cloud; he seems to literally expand with some rising internal pressure he can scarcely contain. She feels he will yell or grab her. But his legs haul him backward instead. *"Chao co,"* he says. *"Chao co,* Lan." The roaring jeep takes him, tires spinning from the muddy gravel to the road, and she is left there in the glaring, sweltering sun to care or not to care.

"GI is Lan's servant," says Madamne Lieu, speaking in her growling way. "Love of Lan makes the GI a servant of her pussy."

"I don't know him."

"He comes here."

"Maybe."

"You lie."

"No. Some babysan steal my money, Lieu."

"Who?"

"I don't know. I don't know. Nothing." Unsettled over the gnawing space in her that doesn't fill with this strange GI's name, she grunts and goes around the corner to the path that runs along the side of the building and into trees, a slant of dirt. At the bottom there is a plank that rises to the privy built on stilts sunk into cloudy, muddy water. All wood, it stands on its fastidious little legs as if in repugnance of the fetid water. The stilts are black and gnarled. An old woman now occupies the stall. The knob of her head wrapped in a cloth is visible above the gate that gives only slight privacy. She smiles at Lan and says the day is lovely, as her urine dribbles in the air. Hit with light, it glitters, splatters. A turd topples through the space of sky between the floor and water, where a swirling movement occurs as responding fish stir the surface. The old woman rises and descends the plank bridge, moving carefully backward on her hands and knees. "My husband," she tells Lan, "says there was fighting and many American things that fly were knocked to the ground. The field was full of them. Like they had been thrown away and no one wanted them at all. What holds them in the sky anyway?"

Lan is staring. At the sight of the water she has been brought back to the morning memory of the dream of drowning. Her? Climbing? Slipping? Falling? Who whispers the thoughts in the brain? As if to pierce the mask of air, the fraud of light, and glimpse, truly, the spirit world—presence or absence—she squints, her head jutting forward like a chicken.

A slight breeze crosses her. Two of her four sisters died of disease when touched by an evil wind. Their swollen stomachs were like sacks of water, distended, with the worms devouring them and filling them until they were gagging, at the start of suffocation. Lan's mother and aunt dragged up wet, squirming worms in fistfuls from the open little mouths. The dead puffy bodies, once beloved, were dropped into holes in the dirt with no ceremony.

She is on the planking now above the water, which is so grimy only faded reflections show upon it. In the hope of hearing her two dead sisters, she had listened quite closely to the air for a long time after their dying. Dark corners intrigued her. When no voices came, she thought of how the infants had said nothing in life, so perhaps their silence was natural enough. Her father's dying was, however, another matter, for he had been loud and full of opinions and stories and poems that he sang.

Now she squats in the footrests that are on either side of the hole in the wood over the water. At the sight of his dead body, a new and unexpected longing, as vague and real as wisps of smoke, had come into her child's mind: she hoped to gain a nearness to him that had been impossible in life; she felt a joyful expectancy. They would be in each other. Free of his labors and worries, would he not float about, hovering often at her ear? Unseen by others, overheard by no one, they would have secrets; his spirit would love her best. She had watched intently as the corpse was washed and dressed in tunic and turban. After rice was slipped in the mouth, the body was lifted to a coffin placed before the family altar. When she bowed with a cup of rice on her palms, she heard him speak, but looked to see her uncle Chie whispering to a neighbor in the corner. Worried now, she frowned and felt a little fear. But the body's possession of the spirit continued, she knew, until the person was in the grave beneath the dirt, listening for the sound of certain prayers the family murmured in the home to call the spirit back. She looked at the body warmly and with wonder, for her father was still inside. Their praying voices would pierce the air, the dirt, his dead skin and bones, and he would hear them. Impatiently, she asked to start the prayers, a loneliness growing in her for her father. Before the burial, offerings of rice alcohol, tea, and sandalwood were made to the altar of the ancestors, where his photograph, selected and placed by her scrupulous uncle, Quach Van Khiem, stood. Her father's expression was somber, formal yet sweet. Imitating the ritual procedures of the professional pallbearers, relatives and friends, all under the guidance of Uncle Khiem, formed and conducted the procession to the grave. Clapping sticks of wood signaled the various movements of the cortege. Her uncles Khiem and Chie carried a miniature altar upon which lay the photograph of her father amid flowers, altar tablets, and burning sticks of joss. Paper money blew about their feet like flowers. Upon completion of the ceremony beside the grave, the family hurried home to say the prayers that would help his soul rise from the grave and fly to the candlelit air of the altar, where the photograph waited, inviting him to return. Lan yearned for the prayers to begin and listened with tightly shut eyes once they did. But with her heart sore and her patience worn raw she could not stay; she ran back to the forest grave site. She would be the first to greet her father. Four young men were drinking tea and wine while hauling about the dirt that would fill the hole. Seeing her arrive, one of them said, "Quach Ngoc Lan is happy at her father's death." She begged them to hurry with their task and, insolently, they slowed their pace. Weeping, she threatened to tell the village chief they were not doing their job. In response, two of them flopped down to rest, while the second pair mockingly tossed clumps of dirt at her. There was little pain in the blows, but as the boys bumped and stained her, the dread that came into her bones made the tears stop and she turned away. She knew suddenly how she would sit in the moonless dark of that night in silence beside the unmoving dirt of her father's grave and the only voice in her head or the air would be her own. For hours the dirt would have covered him, and the prayers, like a drumming of rain, would have run in her head. Where was he? Where? Beside her she would see grass, overhead the sky, all around her trees.

Now, squatting in the privy, she wonders if people and their lives are not like the waste of her body falling through the air to the water, disappearing.

And curiously mixing in her mind, an image beneath an image, the apparition of a child drifts out from a watery gray, a boy who steals, the one who robbed from her. As she descends the planking, he swims forward from some faraway place, and with stealth, he creeps on the path beside the shanty. Cunningly, he peeks in the window to discover some unwatched item of value. She is immobile now on the sloping hillside. She will stop him. Yes. A rat of selfishness absorbed only in himself and what he wants, this boy is a devil. On a table inside sits her purse. His arm slowly moves. She will get him; she will trick him. Reaching as he reaches, her hands will close in his hair. Yelling, he will try to run. Screaming, scolding, she will throw him against the wall, punching, slapping, knocking him down. From the dirt, he will cry as she stomps on his hands. No more stealing. No more. Her kicking feet will break him, stomp him, scrape and bruise his heart. She will squeeze his little prick and balls, that funny little sack. What an agony he will feel. What a howling his little voice will make. What a deserved pain.

16

The small boy has taken Whitaker's hand to guide him through the frantic traffic and across the street to a café where the food is fit to eat. Whitaker has been warned about getting dysentery from the Vietnamese food and cooking. At camp he'd been given the name of a couple of places rumored to be halfway safe, but he couldn't find them. The boy's funny little nose is narrow at the bridge and wide at the nostrils, and his black hair, dirty and unhealthy looking, dangles in bangs above his large, serious eyes. Led docilely along by this child's tugging fingers locked around his thumb, Whitaker feels foolish. Upon their meeting, the boy said, "You boucoup GI," meaning he thought Whitaker very large. The boy is frail; Whitaker will feed him. Because there is no sidewalk, they must step over and around holes, pockets of garbage pink with rot and sprinkled with colored paper, knots of cloth stained with paint or blood. A broken branch catches his foot, and Whitaker stumbles slightly. The street is crowded, a multitude of people walking up and down it and both ways across it while trucks, uncountable scooters—Vespas, Hondas—and a kind of couch on wheels propelled from behind by a man on a bicycle are all squalling and honking in every direction. Battling the din as if desperate to be heard, music blasts from bars along the street. The gaudy glare of their interiors, like the rambunctious rock and roll, squeezes into the oncoming dusk.

The boy says to Whitaker, "Every person dinky dow."

"Creezy," says Whitaker.

An alleyway leads to a wet and glittering dimness, a hive of shanties. From out of this gloom come three laughing GIs in jungle fatigues marked with the winged blue patches of the 173rd Airborne. They were in the shit recently, a big, bloody battle everybody heard about. As Whitaker looks after them, the boy jerks on his hand, turning him sharply to rattle through a curtain of beads on strings covering a doorway in a faded red wall beyond which light increases and many colorful tables stand amid loud music—Martha and the Vandellas. "Okay, GI, can do chop-chop numba one," says the boy.

"No get sick."

A slim young waiter wearing black trousers and a white dress shirt approaches, talking excitedly, his eyes on the boy who clings more tightly to Whitaker's hand and spits out a string of loud Vietnamese words. When the waiter's eyes leap from the boy to the door, Whitaker understands. "Oh, no," he says. "No, no; he stays."

"Wait, GI. You no 'stand." The waiter is grinning. "Wait. Okay."

"I 'stand."

"No babysan can come. Numba ten. Beg money. Not nice. Other GI no like boucoup babysan talk GI—him eating— 'Gimme money, gimme money.' Numba ten."

"No sweat."

"Maybe steal."

"No. Babysan come me, sit me, no beg money; I go, he go. No sweat."

"Cannot do. No babysan."

"Shit, too," Whitaker says.

A second Vietnamese, slightly older than the first, steps from behind the bar, wiping his hands on a towel, brushing his fingers through his hair. A sentence of Vietnamese spurts from his lips along with a buzzing little laugh, and the first young man pivots to leave while the new arrival, the older man, remains, nodding to Whitaker. "You want buy food for babysan?"

"Yeah. Right."

"Okay. You sit down, okay?"

"Fine."

"You watch babysan, he don't steal, okay?"

As they are guided to a table against the wall, the boy says something to the man that sounds friendly and receives a seemingly friendly reply. When the man is gone, Whitaker says, "Nobody like babysan."

"No sweat."

"Babysan steal."

"I no steal."

"You lie."

"No. No *sau*. Xom numba one."

"I steal," Whitaker says.

"What?"

"Sure."

"Eeeeaaaaa?" Amazement lights the whole of his face. "GI? Steal?" And he rocks back, giggling, cocking the chair up on its legs.

"For sure."

"You *sau*. Boucoup *sau*."

"No."

"Troi oi," he sings. *"Troi duc oi."*

The waitress, as tiny as a child and too shy to look directly at them, arrives to take their order of two steaks with french fries, one Bommniba Beer 33, one orange soda. A second waitress sits at the bar. The sleek black of her hair is pulled into a ponytail, and her exact, lovely body is garbed in a blouse and black slacks that taper to the pink of her ankles. She sits at the bar studying a glass of Coke that stands before her. Two waiters occupy a table at the rear. There is an odor of cooking and a deeper, more pervasive stench of backed-up sewage. Whitaker whistles, looking at the girl. Off duty since noon because he pulled guard duty the preceding night, he was laid in the middle of the afternoon, but she was old, wrinkled, and skinny. He would like a young one. A real pretty young one.

The beer and soda arrive along with a pair of green-tinted glasses filled with ice like chunks of crystal containing delicate, explosionlike designs. Drinking beer that leaves an aftertaste and bits of grain on his tongue, Whitaker says, "You live Bien Hoa?"

"For sure. Xom. Me, Xom. Me."

"Xom?"

"Name-me."

"Xom? Name you Xom? Creezy."

"No."

"For sure. Creezy. Xom-Xom," Whitaker says. "Creezy. Xom-Xom."

"You gimme cigarette, okay?"

"For sure." He taps one loose and the kid plucks it out. Whitaker takes one for himself and they light up. He drinks deeply to finish this fourth or fifth bottle of beer for the day— or is it the seventh or ninth? He doesn't know, yelling for more, and when the steaks arrive, they are of a medium thickness, cooked to a deep charcoal darkness. The fibers of the muscle show as wrinkles in its surface. A slice of tomato lies at the edge of the plate. The potatoes, burned and crisp at the tips, are soft at their centers. Xom goes cutting and hacking away, greedy with his knife, while Whitaker, watching, is pleased. He is warmed by the impression that he is a great, bright gift sent into the boy's desolation. The fork hauling meat toward Xom's open mouth stops; his dark eyes glint with a fearful look aimed past Whitaker and toward something behind him. A hand falls on Whitaker's shoulder, brown, the knuckles deeply wrinkled. He sees the fingers lying there, the pink skin near the nails, and up he looks into the bloodshot eyes of Rasputin.

"You ugly," Rasputin says.

"Goddamn," Whitaker says. "Goddamn." Elation is large in his throat.

"Friend you, huh?" Xom asks.

"Yeah, yeah."

"Numba one," says the boy and the worry leaves his face as he goes back to eating.

"C'mon, sit down," says Whitaker. "Lemme buy you a beer."

"No friend to me," Rasputin says, looking at Xom. "Don't have no friend in the world." Taking a chair from an adjacent table, he eases down, melting into the shape of it. "I ain't got much time to spend with you, Whitaker. I got too many moves to make. My, my, look at that boy chow down. He's a hungry boy, Whitaker. You got you a starving child."

"Xom," says Whitaker.

And the boy looks up, alert to detect the nature of the thing expected of him.

"Say hello to my friend."

"Okay. For sure. Hello, GI."

"Hello, funny face."

"Eat," says Whitaker.

"Numba one," says Xom.

"Where you at?" Whitaker says to Rasputin. "Where'd they put you?"

"I'm at the air base, man. I'm some goddamn colonel's driver. How you like that shit? I drive that motherin' jeep all up and down the streets. We important, him and me."

"What about the other guys? They there, too? You ever see any a the other guys?"

"Everybody all over hell, Whitaker. Whole unit broke up. Got picked to pieces hangin' around that 90th Replacement. Ain't no such unit no more like we come over here with. Bunch a replacement parts now. Not that we was much of a unit. Gone. Shipped all over everywhere. They in Saigon. Couple poor bastards in Di An. Kramer, for one. They in Cu Chi. Where you?"

"Long Binh. Me and Rowe out there."

"Rowe. That crazy nigger out there?"

"Sure. We left together, me and Rowe. First of everybody."

"I don't remember that."

"Yeah, yeah."

"You and Rowe to blame, then."

"I guess."

"I like this war, you know that, Whitaker? This is nice motherin' war, I got me old friends I can bump into and reminisce with, I ain't been in it all that long at all. How you like the war, Whitaker?"

"Fine."

"Sure. It's a real good war, makin' you and me friends. You know what, when you finished, Whitaker, I got an errand, you wanna come with me? Back in the alleys. Huh? You been back there yet, back in them alleys?"

"Not around here."

"Shit, it nice back there. You been laid?"

"Sure."

And Xom makes a happy sound, a burp of pleasure not quite laughter, his eyes glittering at them over the glass of bright orange drink. "You want fuck-fuck, GI?"

"Little, bitty pimpy man," says Rasputin.

"I had this old goddamn grandmother, I think, man," says Whitaker. "I was lookin' for witches, you know, maybe she was one, all the while I was humpin'."

"Ain't you somethin'," Rasputin says. "Maybe we got some time you best go check out the Rin-Tin-Tin bar. Do you some good."

Xom, who has been listening closely, nods knowingly at the name of the bar. "I know numba one. Reen-Teen-Teen bar. Same-same dog can kill you."

"C'mon," Rasputin says, "pay what you owe, we'll go on my little errand." Dragging his leg as he rises, his chair rocks and nearly goes clattering to the tile floor but Whitaker lunges, catching it. A waiter scurries over to be paid. When they exit,

Whitaker and Xom find Rasputin standing at the edge of the street, both hands hanging limply from the rims of his pockets as he wobbles a little, his head tilted to let him look skyward. The sight of him compels both Xom and Whitaker to trace the line of his gaze with their own.

"I got to get my smokes," Rasputin says.

Whitaker sees nothing of interest in the smudged and stagnant blankness overhead.

"Let's go get my smokes, Whitaker."

"Can cigarette him, okay," Xom is saying, pointing across the street to a man behind a stall built on two wagon wheels with stacks of cigarette cartons on display. The boy waggles his fingers to make his idea clear.

"I want go alley, man," says Rasputin.

"Oh."

"You 'stand. Back alley."

"Marri-you-anna. Sure. I know." And his serious, old man's head bows.

"Is that what you want?" Whitaker says.

"Deed I do." His eyes are bloodshot; stains show on the inner edge of his lower lip. "You gettin' into it, my man?" he says to Whitaker. "You like your pot, Whitaker?"

"Sure."

"You ever had it?"

"Couple times."

They are strolling now, the boy between them. Whitaker lights up and hands another Pall Mall to Xom.

"I like a good reefer, man," Rasputin is saying. "Back home I'd come in from work, just put on this whole stack a records, climb inta bed smokin'. Be floatin'. Trouble with broads that way sometimes. One day I want pussy, next day I don't. Broad

don't understand that always. Yeah. Lord, I hate to be both-
ered. It always happenin'. Hassle. Hassle. Last night I'm with
this ho. Late in the day. In come these ARVNs. This ho sit-
tin' on my lap, we talkin', you know, both silly, these ARVNs
start talkin' gook talk to her, she kinda shittin' all over 'em
the way she lookin' at 'em. They kinda stompin' around, their
skinny asses all bent outta shape. I don't like the feelin' I'm
gettin'. Only thing clear is how she thinks they are shit. Then
this other GI come up to me sayin', 'Better let her go, man.
You don't want her gettin' hurt.' I don't know what he's sayin'.
I ain't even stoppin' her. I ain't stoppin' nobody. I don't care
what she does. How come they all gotta hassle me? Don't she
know the situation? Fuckin' gooks, crazy, man. 'Go on with
'em,' I tell her, so she goes vicious on my ass, yelling at me,
and yellin' at them, too. They're drunk. She fuckin' hates them
little men. We in a war, man, all on the same side. Let 'em fuck
her, I say. You see what I'm sayin'?"

Entering the narrow alley, they are immediately in mud
and a further diminishment of light. The water that fills the
imprints left by their footsteps stinks of waste and rot. On either side are houses built of dark, decaying wood, hunks and
slabs of tin, occasional stone walls and tile roofs. Some appear
to have been set on bases of concrete.

"People used to throw rocks at me," says Rasputin. "Used
to come from far and near. I was telephone man in the city a
Watts, that's L.A., and them people crazy out there, they got
no entertainment. I'd be up there, workin', doin' my job, pretty
soon I'd hear some somebody callin'—'Telephone man, Telephone man,' and then another one, all these yellin' voices sayin'
it, the word spreadin'. Pretty soon, there be fifteen, twenty,
thirty kids, all kinds, and then they start to throwin' rocks at

me and shootin' rocks out a slingshots, tryin' to knock me off my ladder just to see me fall."

Whitaker chuckles a little.

"Ain't that some shit," says Rasputin. "How come you got me so talkative, Whitaker—tellin' stories like I got a TV in my head. What's happenin' here?"

Xom yanks on Whitaker's sleeve and says, "Numba ten." He looks up at Whitaker. He gestures in the direction they are going and shakes his head. "No, no. GI no, no. *Dung Lai.*"

"No sweat," Rasputin tells him.

"What's he babblin' about?" Whitaker wants to know.

"Off-limits back here. But we just *di di* in and *di di*-the-fuck-*mau* out."

They continue in silence for a time down the cluttered lanes of shanties, sheds, and houses until the alley is no more than a pathway. The mud makes wet, sucking sounds with their every stride and the stench is constant. People on porches wear cotton or silk pajamas and stare. A naked infant sits on the edge of a cistern while her mother pulls up buckets and dumps them into a large urn. The child watches the three of them pass, her small hands stuffed into her mouth. The mother, after glancing at the child, squints at Whitaker and Rasputin. She frowns at Xom, then picks up the child and squats with her knees pressed up into her armpits, her buttocks almost against the ground.

"Just around the corner," says Rasputin. He turns at the edge of a building, and the rutted lane before them shows leaden light on patches of water. He looks up and sees a smoky sky, a gray moon. Conversations within the crammed, almost interconnected houses mingle in the air around them. The thin walls keep little contained. Xom, bowing, grabs a stick that he taps on the ground as they walk.

Materializing from the murk between two shanties, a pair of GIs go by in silence.

"Just be a minute, Whitaker," says Rasputin, stepping toward a doorway set deep in a rough concrete frame. "I ain't gonna be no more than a second," he says, rapping softly on the door.

"Hey, GI," Xom says, "I go now."

Rasputin, at the side of Whitaker's vision, vanishes. "What?" he says to Xom while looking after Rasputin.

"I go now."

"Go?"

"You gimme money."

"What?"

"Money, GI. For sure. I go my house, no hab money, Mama-san-me gimme numba ten—numba fuckin' ten."

"Give you money?" says Whitaker.

"For sure, for sure. Friend-me."

"For sure," says Whitaker, "but no give money."

"Yes, yes."

"Buy you food, buy you orange. No give money."

"C'mon," says Xom. "Fuck."

"Hey."

"You friend-me, c'mon. Cheap Charlie."

"Talk numba ten, Xom."

"You no gimme money, you numba ten. Cheap Charlie."

"Hey."

"Fuck you, numba goddamn fuckin' ten, GI. Gimme money!" Emotion has him rigid, yet the words are delivered in a frightened, shaking voice. "You *sau*. Boucoup *sau*!"

"No, *sau*."

"Boucoup *sau*!"

"Xom-Xom," Whitaker says. "Friend-me. For sure." He speaks carefully, softly, out of his own dismay.

"Must hab money!" Xom cries in rage and panic. His ragged shirt, Whitaker notices for the first time, is marked with little blue cowboys, red and blue horses. Xom is more bone than body in his cutoff unhemmed shorts; his feet bare, he trembles, and with a sudden cry that Whitaker cannot understand, he flees off down the alley, leaving Whitaker bewildered. Motionless, rocking a little from foot to foot, he stares at the dark, realizing in the passing moods of several cloudy moments that he is very drunk. Xom will reappear, he believes; Xom will apologetically return. He'll make a joke. Maybe Whitaker will give him some money. Puffing a cigarette he does not remember lighting, he finds Rasputin beside him. Beyond Rasputin, an old woman stands in the open doorway; she has the silhouette of a hawk to the frowning, squinting Whitaker. Coals burn in the black beyond her.

"You get it?" Whitaker says.

Rasputin grins. His chuckle is a deep, happy, whining sound going off in his throat. "The kid gone?"

"Yeah."

"Them kids gotta scramble, man."

A candle moves across a window behind Rasputin's head and Whitaker strains to glimpse the hand that holds it. Tossing aside his cigarette, he lights the one Rasputin offers, for the air is sweet already with the smoke of Rasputin's exhalations. The cigarette, thin and wrinkled, more flat than round, is a Kent that has been emptied and repacked. "Now we gonna go get some sweet ass that's young," Whitaker says, hoping he sounds and looks experienced. He takes his first drag deep, a warm wind to blow through his mind, down and around with his blood. He pants for some additional air to help draw the thick smoke in; it is slightly acrid in his nostrils; he feels needles in his lungs, as he watches the joint go back and forth. It's dark, he sees. Night. He and Rasputin are walking, and then in a different place, having strayed a ways among the shanties with Rasputin telling stories to which Whitaker scarcely listened. In the strangeness of his mind, wavy and slow, he is graceful and cool. He reaches way back, and punches Rasputin hard in the back of the head and watches him fall; he yells, "You're it, Rasputin," and goes running off to skid in mud and hide among chickens, his back to the wall of a house, his arms embracing the large urn behind which he has crouched for concealment. Chickens squawk crazily and rock on their stubby legs. He sees the bumps like blisters all over their ugly legs and feet. Their knees are bending wrongways. All exploding feathers, one bounces slowly in the air. Where's Rasputin? Does Whitaker know? Yes, he thinks, remembering the long, slow flight of his fist through the air. Did he do that graceful blow for a reason? The stench of the chickens is strong: their old droppings and stale water mix with the decay of half-rotted grain. Grime is embedded in their bodies, he believes, in the filthy fibers of their feathers. He wonders a moment about Rasputin. Yes. His mind seeks to find Rasputin in the complex village taking shape in his imagination, all byways, alleys, lightless shanties. East? North? He tries nooks and crannies, but comes, he thinks, upon Xom, lost and lonely. But when he looks he's all by himself, kneeling somewhere strange with no one near but chickens. He blinks, weary of the game. He glances right, preparing to stand—he will rise to return to the compound to play some poker—and then he is staring into the face of an old man, wrinkled and tawny, tufts of a white, wispy goatee.

Not two feet away from Whitaker, the man's eyes sparkle crazily behind a window of wire mesh, and Whitaker is terrified, while the old man covers his mouth and giggles with great pleasure at the fulfillment of a little joke.

Whitaker leaves hurriedly, hoping to tell Rasputin about this ambush. But he has no idea where Rasputin is. The alleyways wind and twist. He fears he's wandering deeper into the maze of wherever he's walking. The high-pitched chatter inside the little houses is coming less often, growing fainter. Is everybody lying down to go to sleep? The whole of the night becomes quieter and quieter, deeper and darker, until the loud slap of feet brings breathless American voices toward him. They come from out of nowhere, two kids in jungle fatigues, the first one flying by without a word, but the second, bigger, thicker, tells him, "Run, run." Whitaker freezes, wheels, then chases after them. He gets within a yard of the last kid, who's huffing and puffing, "Shit, shit, shit."

Afraid to shout, Whitaker whispers, "What is it? What is it?"

"What?"

"Is it VC?"

"No, man, it's the fucking MPs!"

Relieved, Whitaker is instantly and differently scared. They veer around a corner. The alley zigzags, then straightens out. He passes a lane that runs to the left and sees white-helmeted MPs, at least three or four of them, flash by on a parallel walkway that intersects with the one he's looking down. It's a sweep of the off-limits village. They're hunting down soldiers who've gone AWOL and are hiding out, or anybody they find, because nobody should be there. The two kids in jungle fatigues are climbing a gray corrugated tin fence directly ahead and maybe eight feet high. The one has grasped the top edge and is straining to throw his right leg up and over. The second is jumping for a handhold. The fence shakes and wobbles. As Whitaker runs up, the metal groans under the stress of their attack. With a sudden shrill squeal it collapses. They tumble toward him, and he jumps back to get out of their way. But the fence isn't a fence. It's the wall of somebody's house that they've pulled down. A whole family is sitting there uncovered. Kids, three or four, a woman, the man rising to his feet. There's a steaming black cookstove. It looks like they were having dinner. They're all shouting and screeching, the baby's crying. They're all angry and scolding. Dogs are barking in three or four different directions.

The two GIs scramble past him, saying, *"Xin loi, Xin loi."*

"Sorry," the big one yells.

Whitaker turns to run after them.

17

Way far away and hard to believe at first, traces of car horns and variously pitched engines call to him with hints of which way to go. The whine of Lambrettas, Hondas, and mechanized cyclos; the grumble of jeeps, taxis, trucks, along with the music piped into the night from bars, guide him through the confusion of all those hovels and out into the bright bustle of downtown Bien Hoa. When he steps from the backstreets into the open air, he is sweaty and gasping and insanely thirsty. He bends, his hands on his knees. He wants a cigarette, but has lost his pack. He gratefully locates the nub of grass still in his pocket and salvages one last toke huddled near a wall. When he straightens, it's weird how the first thing he expects to see is Xom and Rasputin. But all he sees is everybody else. He buys a pack of Camels and climbs into the cab of a Lambretta to cruise down the streets of shops and many bars, inside one of which he will find Xom and Rasputin, he is sure. But suddenly, it is sometime later and he is lolling alone in his Lambretta, smoking a cigarette, while fields drift past beyond the trees alongside the road. The moon is yellow. He has a slight headache and is very very thirsty. Maybe too thirsty to live. It scares him to have drunk so much and smoked on top of it. The fear spins a little, floats in his head, falls to his stomach. He'll get killed one of these days, dead in a ditch, a corpse, beautiful no more, shit. Glancing at his watch—9:05—he pats his pocket to feel the comfort of the knife he carries folded there. He slips it out, keeping it hidden after levering the tip open against his thigh. He looks at the driver's silhouette and thinks of the road and the wheels turning under them. Then he hears a surprising sound. It's a chorus of girls' voices, somewhere ahead in the dark. He leans out the slatted side of the cab. Before him on the right-hand edge of the road, figures dart through the frame of light cast from the windows of a shanty. Another light appears, narrow, quivering, the wan projection of what he thinks is a Lambretta parked on the shoulder, the engine sputtering to life. Then the poor beam of Whitaker's vehicle touches the scene, revealing three girls bidding farewell to a GI who is climbing onto the back of a motor scooter. They seem to have come from a building that sits in a clearing just off the road. He thinks he remembers passing it in daylight, and what he remembers is blue stone situated in white gravel. On impulse, grinning Whitaker says, "Stop. Dung Lye," to his driver as the girls yelp and hop about the scooter beginning to move. Whitaker has a peculiar feeling. Without plan or map to chart the night, he may have had a stroke of luck. Will he find a little cutie china doll? Blasted on beer and pot, wayward amid all those back alleys, he is here. The lingering beer and grass have soaked his blood in self-infatuation. He feels, with reasonless excitement, at the center of a big accomplishment.

When the scooter has buzzed away fifty feet or so, the taller two girls move side by side toward the house, while the third, the smallest, dances after the departing scooter, and then jumps up and down until nothing is any longer visible down the road.

Whitaker wonders briefly about the late hour—dare he risk taking the time to get laid now? And then he worries that these girls aren't whores, but just girls. But wouldn't whores be the only ones saying good-bye to a GI in the dark at this hour? He has paid the Lambretta driver. The engine throttles up behind him. "Hello," he says to the remaining girl. She turns. *"Chao co,"* he says. "Hello."

Though skinny and slouching, a little boyish in her build, she seems an amazingly beautiful whore dressed in blue slacks and a pale blue shirt that hangs loose about her hips. His earlier excitement calls to him with its claim that it looks like his hope for good luck is coming true. Or will she tell him to go on and just dee-dee on down the road, no more ass tonight. "You got a beer?" he says.

"For sure," she says. "C'mon."

"Coke, too."

"Okay. For sure."

As they enter the little house, Whitaker pauses in the doorway to glance down the darkened road. He feels a little regret and wonders if his watch is right. Curfew is ten o'clock. Out beyond that time will mean he must stay out all night or risk being reported for returning late. And what if the VC find him naked and humping? Well, they'd shoot his ass? He should go back. Or what if MPs haul his naked ass off to the clink, the motherfucking clink?

The girl is grinning at him from across the room, having gone away and come back with Bommniba Beer 33 in a bottle and Coke in a can. Her buoyancy puzzles him, as does her beauty, and he begins to believe it's all a mistake. He starts to doubt his good luck, the odds shifting toward his earlier worry that she is no whore. She has opened both the bottle and can for him, and the ice in which they were kept has left them cold, wet, and flecked with sawdust. Taking them from her hands, he decides she's just too happy go lucky; her eagerness and enthusiasm can't belong to somebody who's been screwing all day. Now he searches for the other girls, the replacements, expecting them to enter, old and ugly, the ones he'll get to fuck after being aroused by this pretty one.

"Okay," she says, "c'mon," pointing to a bench along the wall. He obeys and sits and she departs. A moment later, he glimpses her through an open window between the rooms. He guzzles the Coke, takes a long drink of beer, and glowers at the floor. He cannot believe money will be enough to buy him the loveliness of this girl. She will vanish like Sharon; he could not have Sharon. He does not get loveliness. The others will appear. That was the routine in all the bars: young girls lured and aroused you, their ripe, sweet softness the dream that got you going. Then you were ready, swollen and eager, and the young girl was gone—slipped away like air. The back-alley room where you went was full of old women, ugly girls. In them you rubbed yourself into release, ignoring their bitterness and boredom.

Mired in these thoughts, their dismal claim on his future, he is surprised when the girl returns to sit upon his lap. Then her hand fits into his crotch; the fingers seek to cradle, then pet, his balls. She whispers, *Troi oi.* And he says nothing, looking at the wall of cracked stone beside the makeshift window through which he can see the neighboring house where maybe the Mamasan lives. The tingling in his crotch is sweet; still he does not believe. He thinks to put his hand to her tit and finds a handful of largely padded bra.

"Yeah, yeah." She smiles. "You like me do prick you. Maybe long-time. All right. Do fuck-fuck all night."

"You," he says again, pointing at her.

"Lan," she says. "For sure. No sweat."

"Lan."

"Can do fuck-fuck me. Lan."

What is it that forbids him to believe he will have her? He will spend money anytime for the body of a woman. To spend money for the body of a woman seems to him a theft in which he is clever and devious and enviably bold. He believes that he knows that when they bargain for dollars, they don't know what they're doing; they are settling for less than what they secretly know they secretly want, though what that is, exactly, he doesn't know and doesn't have to know. He feels it and believes what he feels, just as he believes in theft and unanswered questions, and paying as little attention as possible to his own thinking.

Now the two other girls shuffle through the room and he examines them with curiosity, aware for the first time of something strange in their coloration, an oddity in their features. "No Vietnam," he says and they giggle under his scrutiny.

"Indian," says his girl. "Sisters. Same-same."

"Indians?"

"For sure."

They are big breasted as Americans, their hair lacquered stiff with PX hair spray. Indians from India. The mystery of their presence here makes him feel that the world is huge and as full of surprises as a crackerjacks box. It makes him want to give an Indian war whoop, while in the corner the two girls appear to be preparing for departure; their purpose in the room is to transfer small articles from a shelf to a suitcase.

Lan has his hard prick lying up against his belly where she is petting it with her thumb, her body shielding the activity from the others' view. That she is so thoughtful, so private, pleases him, though his bulging trousers could hardly be a cause for embarrassment here, even if seen. Still, he's glad. "Can do short-time now, okay?"

"No, no," she says.

He feels doomed the instant he hears her denial and the urge to throw her across the room twitches in his hands.

"Long-time," she says. "Do you long-time. All night, okay? Sleep me." And to convince him she gives the tip of his prick an affectionate little twist that makes him swallow hard and blink.

A jeep pulls onto the space of ground in front of the shanty, headlights winking out before the wheels cease. The two girls, giggling, dart out the door.

"Boucoup GI," says Lan.

They enter, tough-looking, stocky young men, who nod to Whitaker with Lan sitting on his lap. He puts his arm across her thigh so his fingers dangle against her crotch.

She whispers, close to him: "Sleep all night, okay. *Ti ti,* they *di di mau.*"

The two girls, having gone for beer, return and settle into the arms of the new arrivals, while Whitaker, giving in to the residue of the pot and the gaseous lulling alcohol of his beer, begins to drift. Sitting with his prick pleasantly hard, the urge to ride is arousing but peaceful because satisfaction is certain. As he drifts, he dreams and circles around the question of staying through the night. Not only might he die by Vietcong, but should his absence from camp be discovered, he would be AWOL. He needs to go. Right now. It's not too late. Even if he ends up with some kind of punishment for being out past curfew, he'd be better off than ending up dead. It's good advice, and he knows it, but it seems intended for somebody else. He thinks of being AWOL, and likes the idea of the label beside his name, the sense it gives of who he is. Just then he starts, called by something he's picked up on in the air without even knowing he was looking. It pulls him from his thoughts into the room, where he recognizes nervousness in the other two GIs. They laugh too loudly. Whitaker asks where they're from, meaning the name of their military unit, and they tell him, "Louisiana." They wear MACV patches. They smile and eye each other, but their girls do not like them. Whitaker can feel it somehow, like he's reading everybody's mind. Wonderfully confident now in the luxury of Lan having chosen him, he feels how much better he is than these strangers. One of the big Indian girls, shifting clumsily for comfort, slips and with a loud yell plops to the floor. Whitaker laughs heartily, and while she struggles up, babbling and embarrassedly scolding the GI who dropped her, everyone giggles and looks at one another as if to say how happy they all are to be there together.

Later Lan enters from the shadows of the back room into the flickering light of the front and Whitaker sees the pink of her panties bulging through the side of her slacks where the zipper isn't holding. He will be there soon, he thinks. But then her hand leaps to cover the hole in her clothing, and shame flashes in her eyes. She tugs the shirttail down to cover the pinkness. Whitaker doesn't understand and then he thinks he does. But it's hard to believe that she's embarrassed by the shabbiness of her clothes, that she went to the trouble of keeping her long shirt untucked all evening to conceal a broken zipper. She is bent near him, whispering now that she is going away for a minute. Will he stay the night? One thousand five hundred Ps.

"Yes," he says. "You."

"No sweat. I go. Tee-tee, I come back." Before departing she delivers a smiling statement to the Indian girls, who grin knowingly to each other and giggle and nod.

Whitaker, watching her shifting buttocks as she leaves, is drinking beer and thinking, I'll fix her transmission. I'll change her oil. I'll look right down her carburetor's throat and aim my flashlight and move the fuckin' throttle linkage and watch the gas spray until the throat is wet. Whitaker sees Lan below him as a sleek, fierce auto; he squeezes a tit to change a gear. He jams his pedal to her floor and, fingers twisting in her hair, drives her down a sweating, squealing two lane.

"Hey," says one of the Louisiana boys, "you come here a lot?"

"Yeah," says Whitaker.

"She your girl?"

"Yeah."

"She sure is a good one."

At that instant, she passes across the open doorway between the rooms, a metal basin and towel balanced in her hands.

"She's gonna take a bath," says the shorter Louisiana boy incredulously.

"That's right," says Whitaker.

"Ain't that somethin'," he says. "Takes good care of herself for you. That's good. Keeps herself clean."

"You ain't ever been here before, huh?" says Whitaker. "I thought maybe you were good friends with them two girls."

"Oh, no," says one.

The other is standing up, stretching. "Did she say somethin' about you and long-time, if I heard right? Don't you worry about gettin' your throat cut sleepin' out all night around here? I don't think I could sleep so good just gooks around."

"Yeah, and what about bed check in your unit?"

"I got an overnight pass," Whitaker lies, and from the skepticism puckering the mouth of one and the envy in the gaze of the other, he takes a warning. They resent him. In their bitterness, might they notify his unit of his absence?

"You don't have no overnight pass to stay here. Not here, man."

"Nobody asks me where I stayed when I get back. They ain't gonna come here lookin' for me, are they?"

"Whatsamatter," says the shorter one, his brow furrowing. "You sound pissed. We're just talkin'."

Whitaker nods. These two don't even know what unit he's with. "Sure," he says.

While they go through a ritual of departure that consists of squeezing the big girls' tits and promising loudly to return early tomorrow, Whitaker wanders outdoors to piss in the bushes along the pathway beside the house. A truck rumbles past, burying briefly the sounds of insects and occasional crying geckos. His urine spatters on leaves. The pathway before him leads to the rear of the house. He thinks of walking carefully upon the worn dirt sprinkled with stones to maybe get a glimpse of Lan bathing. He finds her naked in moonlight that cuts across her narrow hips, putting her legs in darkness. Beside her the dented silver basin contains foggy water, a white bit of shimmering soap. Beyond her is the jungle gloom diminished here and there by dampened leaves or branches catching light.

When he returns to the road, the two GIs are in the jeep. The girls stand beside it, smiling. Whitaker ambles to the shanty entrance. Standing in the doorway as the jeep starts up with everyone waving and chatting away, he feels as if he is saying good night to guests who have paid a visit to his home. It's been a little party and now the guests are leaving in their car. "Bye-bye," says Whitaker. "Nice you could come by."

Before the jeep has traveled far enough to vanish in the dark, the girls have turned away to seize their baskets, purses, and suitcases. In a moment, they're gone, too, hurrying down the road in the opposite direction. Whitaker, with Lan, who has come to stand beside him wearing white cotton pajamas, her long thick hair hanging loose, feels his prick stir and lust mixes with a funny fear and loneliness he does not understand. The silence, comprehensive as sleep, is strange, as if he has never heard a rural night before. She tugs his hand to draw him inside. She touches his prick and makes a kind of clucking, maternal sound, as if in pity of his funny body. Will the VC kill him in the night? Is the source of his gloom the feeling that the departure of that jeep was the departure of all jeeps, all trucks and bikes and scooters, and now he will not ever leave? He looks at Lan but learns nothing except how she is truly not so lovely as he thought, but merely young. Why is he in this place alone with only gooks around?

"You pay mamasan," she says.

"Okay."

"One thousand five hundred."

"Yes."

Their presence everywhere around him is the loneliness he feels, surrounded by their strangeness. Each face is a variation on all the others, their language a silence he does not understand. Like alien trees in an alien forest endlessly duplicating one another, they show him nothing of himself. Lan calls out a sentence in her language; his fear increases.

"Lan," he says, as Mamasan appears, a squint-eyed old woman twisted by some fault in her spine. She grins at Whitaker, says "Hello. One thousand five hundred Ps you sleep Lan all night."

He pays. Two boys shadowed by a wraithlike old man arrive from an adjacent shanty to stand in the dimness. Mamasan mutters at them. They all go out the back door. There are other shanties, Whitaker now sees, peering after them, a number that's hard to determine, wood and straw out near the point where the paddies turn the land soft. Moonlight skitters through the trees. It touches and loses the four silent figures disappearing down that trail.

"What's going on?" says Whitaker.

Lan tells him, "No sweat. Sit down. Have a beer."

To assert himself, he remains standing and leans against the wall, thinking of how he has come to settle here on this grubby floor in a falling-down shanty beside a road between jungle and more jungle in a war—and is this what smart men did, men of daring, Parnelli Jones, A. J. Foyt? Is this smart, Whitaker? Or is it dumb?

The small boy with no shirt returns carrying the headboard of a bed. An instant later, the second boy enters dragging a wooden object like a miniature football goalpost. In the moonlight, the old man staggers on the trail. He balances a slatted rectangle of wood on top of his head. Whitaker stares in amazement; children and old men are walking up and down that trail like goddamn elves, like goddamn fucking elves to get him a bed so he can screw a whore. It's like a demented Disney movie, and he's in it.

Aided by one of the boys, the old man manages to fit his burden through the door. The boys scamper about, assembling the bed. The old man stands, panting a moment. Lan climbs upon the bed to attach a mosquito net to several hooks and nails in the wall. She stretches the bottom toward the end of the bed but it doesn't reach and she gives up. The net hangs, a darker swirl, not quite color, in the little light. Mamasan limps as she leaves, blowing out candles, and the old man and children follow.

The mat Lan unrolls to cover the wooden slats of the bed is a tan weave without design.

While Whitaker undresses, Lan lies upon the bed holding on her belly the candle that is the only light they have. Whitaker sits to untie his boots and her hand comes around his hip to stroke his cock.

"Maybe VC come fini me," he says. "I am sleeping."

"No sweat."

"I am sleeping."

"No. VC numba ten."

"For sure."

In his underwear he walks to a chair where he neatly organizes his clothes before hauling the chair nearer the bed. Knife in hand, he pries the blade open until there's a loud click as it locks; Lan sits up with widened eyes, a yelp of alarm.

"No, no," she says, and she is afraid of him. The terror transforms her small body.

"VC," he says.

"No VC. Me numba one," she says. "Numba one."

He means to dramatize the pointlessness of her fear by waving the knife down through the air until it enters the dirt and sticks there as if in a sheath. Should it be needed, it will be ready, he thinks, while other smarter channels in his brain show him VC shooting his head off as he sleeps. Or stepping in to blast him as he humps away. When he faces her, she extinguishes the candle with a quick puff of breath before squirming out of her pajama bottoms and taking his prick in her fingers. While he looks at her to find some sign of her real mood, she strokes his balls, and lies back. He reaches up under the cotton blouse to find a tit. He decides to arouse her a little with his finger. There is no hair, all smoothness and bone under cool skin until the opening that is wet and deep and hot—he thrusts a little, rubs, aching in his stomach, in his throat, all the while watching her expression for an indication of his effect. And then his brain receives a message: some power in the heat of her has raced secretly, deeply into him he is coming. His seed is on the move. Too late he tries retreat. It spills and spits into the mat while he, straining against this loss, is filled with such tension and denial he feels nothing. The muscles are all in contradiction. He flops upon his back and lays there staring at a gecko spread-eagled on the ceiling while a mosquito buzzes at his nose. The net is poor. So little does his stupid, sorry-assed mistake show on him that a moment later, while he is immobile and depressed, she nudges his hand with her crotch. She wants to do her job. "You do fuck-fuck, GI," she whispers. "Okay? We sleep. Do fuck-fuck me. I sleep."

"No sweat," he says, disappointed beyond anger. "You sleep now."

"Sleep now?"

"Yeah."

"No do fuck-fuck. I sleep?"

"Okay."

"Numba one."

When he awakens, she has thrashed across the bed to the other side near the wall. He doesn't even look at his watch. Sleep has left his head full of dirt and sand, a blowing dust, and he feels like crying, he's such a fuckup. He carefully parts her legs, then kneels above her before she stirs. Her eyes open and she says, "Oh, GI." He tells her he has no prophylactic, no rubber. His calmer mind now thinks of such things, but he's ready to risk VD. She shrugs and, touching his erect prick says, *"Troi oi,"* and reaches out and produces a rubber from somewhere. She concentrates, unwrapping it and carefully fitting it on him. He decides to kiss her and does as she helps him enter with ease. Kneeling, he cups her buttocks in his palms. This will be better, he thinks and twirls his finger in her ear; she makes a funny face. He kisses her, wondering about all the cocks in her day and what she's done with them. From the inner tissue of her mouth comes a strange taste, the odors of her stomach all rising like smoke off the alien food she eats. But he's feeling a lot, and it's strong and it's turning into more. He rides it through and comes hard and beautiful enough this time to gasp and strain his head away from her, his arching back a sign of his agony to go into her further and deeper, stay longer—what does he want?

When he looks at her, she is waiting alertly to see if he is finished. He slumps off of her. She pats his cheek, turns on her side. "Sleep now. Okay."

"Okay."

However, he is unable to and lying there he smokes half a dozen cigarettes and feels very sad. After a while, he wakes her to ask her to get him a beer. She shuffles off and returns, bottle in hand, hot as the very air. The beer brings no pleasure; it makes him thirstier, but he doesn't complain. Lifting it toward the ceiling, he tries to focus on the moon out the window through the brown of the glass. I am Joe Whitaker, he thinks. Whitaker. Joseph. And I come from . . . somewhere . . . anywhere . . . with a banjo on my knee. The sun's so hot . . .

When his watch shows 4:00 AM, he rises and dresses in eerie

half-light while she sleeps, unmoving, and he wonders what she thinks of being a whore. From the limits of his skull he tries to pierce the bone of hers. She sleeps with simple, animal ease. His stomach growls. He feels a changing of pressure in his bowels that is shifting gas. Quietly, he farts.

He bends to look out the square hole cut into the wall to serve as a window. He's getting anxious to leave. Soon laborers will wander the roads, and with this start of the day's routines, Lambrettas will appear. One will stop for him and haul him through the leaden silver of the morning. He will arrive in ghost-gray light to pass the bunkers, guards, and checkpoints of the gate. Crossing fields and passing the tents of other units, traversing the motor pool, he will shower, shave, and go to work.

Lan wakes, blinking.

"You go now?"

"Yeah," he says.

"You come back."

He smiles, and her response startles him. Scampering to where he stands, she unbuttons his fly and fiddles with his prick, but he is finished now. Not even time for a blow job. "No, no," he says. His single interest has become returning to camp. Nothing in him is any longer drunk or high. Though his rejection hurts her, he guesses, probably seeming an insult, the worry is spreading in him that he will not make it back safely. Now he moves out the door. Pausing ten or so yards into the still-dark street, he finds he has no matches for his cigarette. He looks about. She is in the doorway watching him stand there patting his pockets.

"Hey," she says, "you want a light?" A lantern flickers above her, attached to the wall of the shanty, and it moves as she reaches to take it and amble, grinning at him, onto the road.

"I give you light."

He leans into the candle, aware of her smiling face at the edge of his eye. They are husband and wife in the echoes of this moment; he is off to work. She will cook the dinner, care for the kids. "Okay," he says. "Thank you."

"No sweat. You go Lambretta?"

"Yeah."

When it comes, a gladness springs awake within him. He does not know how she woke in the night to eat an orange and stare at him and think of the legendary Old Man of the Moon who sits in moonlight reading his book in which are recorded the connections that will come between people in the world. Quick and silent as a spider, he puts a web of invisible, rosy threads throughout the world until all people everywhere who are destined to be pairs are linked in a secret, lovely manner. Down through their lives the threads draw the lovers, down the trails and rivers, from city to forest, until they finally meet and love. Holding in her palm a wedge of orange she didn't eat, Lan felt her threads running to the air. The wind had them. No old man anywhere knew of her. Whitaker leaps aboard the Lambretta. He is debris, he knows, a leaf that arrived here on a wind and now, thank god, the gusts that brought him have known enough to return. In the comforting free rhythm of their wings, he rides away.

18

In the dusk, they build the bunker. Their sweat dark with grime, they labor into evening. Whitaker ties off two sandbags packed full. He flops them onto his shoulders, feeling the trickle of sweat on his belly, the dust powdering him. He strides over the ruts left by the treads of the Caterpillars that flattened these fields. The First Infantry Division cleared out the Vietcong and then engineers eliminated the foliage. On a square of slightly higher ground above their tents, the bunker is being constructed. The muscles that ache are high in his shoulders. Pausing at the Lyster bag, he drinks a cup of warm, flat water. It gives no refreshment, but taken in large quantities diminishes the caking dust in his mouth.

The earthen debris being used to fill the bags was delivered by a rumbling old dump truck in the middle of the afternoon.

The mound sprawls near the generator that powers feeble lights hung on tent poles about the area where they work. Four men dig with shovels to fill the bags, a stench of waste and age escaping when lumps are broken open. In the distance, the clank and grind of machinery can be heard. Whitaker is returning for another load. One soldier shovels while another sits holding open the mouth of the bag being filled. Bonefezi, a short, squat soldier, thrusts with his spade and says, "You guys know if this was World War Two, we'd have to do all this in the dark, man."

"It is the dark," says Whitaker.

"No, no."

"Whatta you think it is, the middle a the goddamn afternoon, you jerkoff?" says Griffin, Bonefezi's partner, as the bag in his hands shudders and changes shape with the dirt Bonefezi dumps into it. "Look around, man. It ain't exactly the middle a the afternoon, jerkoff."

"I mean, no lights, asshole. No lights."

"Will you watch where you're pourin' that shit, Bonefezi? You're pourin' that shitty smellin' dirt all over me. Will you watch where you're pourin' it? Can you do that?"

"What's it matter, dirty as you are?"

"Okay, so I'm dirty. Does that mean I want to be filthy? No, it don't mean I wanna be filthy. You're stupid, Bonefezi, do you know that? Just because I'm dirty already, you think I want you to stand there pourin' dirt all over me."

"No, I don't. I don't think you want it on you."

"Why," Whitaker says, "would we have to do this in the dark if it was World War Two, Bonefezi?" He is slinging another forty- or fifty-pound bag onto his shoulder; he will carry the second one dangling at arm's length.

"Because of the airplanes if it was World War Two," Bonefezi says. "We couldn't have no lights like this or we'd probably get an air raid."

"What about if it was Korea?" says Byrn, Whitaker's partner.

"Don't tell me about Korea," Rowe calls to them from where he stands constructing the bunker wall. "I loved it in Korea. Those whores gave blow jobs—they could take you round the whole damn world. All the way and back."

"But what if we was workin' there like we are here now. Could we have lights?" Whitaker asks.

"VC only people in the world crazy enough to fight a war they don't have airplanes," Bonefezi tells them.

"Listen," Whitaker says, "I'll stop by again. We'll chat again."

"That's a good idea."

"See you later."

He watches the funny pattern of his feet in the dirt as he trudges toward Rowe and the bunker, the walls of which are halfway completed. Releasing the bag from his hand, he bows to allow the second to skitter, tugging at his skin, from off his shoulder. A small cloud of dust marks its landing. Before him, the bunker seems a crooked, unstable structure, piercing him with a moment's vision of himself and eight or ten others cowering inside the shuddering walls, the roof leaking a rain of dust from the banging concussion of incoming shells. On his way back he passes Griffin, who balances one bag on his shoulder and drags the other. Mortar or rocket attack is their only threat here. The VC are unlikely to try a full-scale assault on such a place. They might hit a nearby village or prowl the ammo dump stretching across the hillsides on the far side of the highway, in the groove of the valley below them running westward toward Vung Tau. Often, flares sparked in the dark above the crates of ammunition stacked over the terrain of those hills like boxes on a wharf.

Heaving up the burden of another hundred pounds, Whitaker sets off, limping a little; his right knee is stiffening where he tore the skin raw when he slipped on gravel while playing tag football. Ahead of him, Rowe works within the bunker walls, where he instructs Doland, who watches closely. Rowe inspects the fit and placement of each bag, attempting to lock them together through their flexibility. Barrels filled with crusted earth, with rock and broken tree limbs form the corners. Rowe sweats heavily and works with the intense and serious concern of a craftsman. He pats and brushes and cleans the bags with the edge of his hand; he slams them furiously with a flat piece of wood to prepare them for the layers that follow.

"Rowe, you eat that shit up, don't you," says Whitaker.

"Love it, Mr. Whitaker. Love to do this work. Anything got to do with hidin' when there gonna maybe be some people shootin', that my kinda work. Mr. Charles comin' up one road, man, I am goin' down the other. I fought my war; I bet you never been shot at, Mr. Whitaker, so you don't have no real appreciation for this bunker. I been shot at, Mr. Whitaker. You and me gonna be huggin' and kissin' them dirty ole walls." The nearest lightbulb wobbles as Rowe bumps a tent pole, and the light wavers on the brown of his flesh, the bumpy stubble of his beard. His thick, open lips pout as he nods to affirm his wisdom. Doland hurries to stabilize their makeshift lamp.

"Whitaker," says a calling voice.

Whitaker turns to find Sergeant Major Wilcox approaching. The man's cleanliness is the first thing Whitaker sees; he doesn't appear to even sweat. Pausing, the sergeant major puts his clipboard against his left knee in order to scribble something on it. The pencil makes a dry sound. "You're on guard tonight, Whitaker. We got to guard our area up here. You're on first shift. Lieutenant Felder is OD. Sergeant Emlin is Sergeant of the guard. Reese's second shift, Roland's third. Two on and four off. You can have the afternoon off tomorrow if you work the mornin'. We got lots to build. You can go down to the village in the afternoon and test the water if you want. Take your galoshes."

"Yes, Sergeant Major."

"You know what I'm talkin' about?"

"Yes, Sergeant Major."

"Then why do you look so fucking stupid? Take your rubbers if you go into town, is what I'm tellin' you. You don't want a dirty dicky, do you?"

"No, Sergeant." Whitaker is blinking to wipe away all evidence of whatever expression might have made him appear stupid.

"That's what I'm sayin'. GI always curious about slant-eyed pussy, you can go see if you like it. I don't mind a boy in my outfit gettin' what he needs, but if he comes down with the clap, I don't like it. I don't like diseases. They make people miss work. That's what I'm tellin' you. You can pass the word to Roland and Reese to wear their galoshes if they're gonna get their dicky wet."

"Yes, Sergeant Major."

"You do right by me, Whitaker, you'll be real happy. We clear?"

"Yes, Sergeant Major."

"You gotta hustle."

"Sergeant Major, what time does first shift start?"

"Real soon, Whitaker."

"Will I have time to shower first?"

"No, no."

"When does it start?"

"Depends on how fast you can get your gear together and report. That's the time first shift starts. You better get a move on. If you wanna be there. Sergeant Emlin and the lieutenant are important people. You can shower after first shift. That'll make you sleep real good. You'll feel real good and clean." Turning away, he strides off toward the bunker where the board in Rowe's hands slams against the bags of the wall and Doland watches.

Artillery booms. An ARVN unit resides down the road. Looking at the sky, Whitaker searches, as if he might see the arcing shells; he feels the smallest of shivers in the earth beneath his feet as the cannons rumble. It's support fire more than likely; artillery launched at request and into requested coordinates; although it might simply be harassment fire: rounds that are sent for no specific reason and with no specific pattern into free-fire zones.

Whitaker pivots, starting to hurry along, thinking of how Sergeant Major Wilcox did not cross with him on that ship. Rowe was on it, and he's run into Rasputin, but the others are scattered all over the place. Once ashore, they traveled as expected to Bien Hoa air base and the 90th Replacement Battalion where they learned they were all being reclassified as "in transit." Rumors flew, and one by one their officers were reassigned. A chubby Spec Five from personnel seemed to enjoy telling them how much he knew and they didn't, how they were going to be shipped out as replacements to random units on the basis of their "military occupational specialty." He couldn't just say "MOS" like everybody else did. Whitaker slept a lot, sluggish in the heat, desperate to get acclimatized. He loitered around the personnel section, trying to pick up any scrap of information that might pertain to him, because those fuckers inside could be deciding to send him anywhere there was a motor pool, which was just about every kind of outfit there was, engineers, artillery, transportation, infantry, you name it. And then one afternoon he and Rowe were told they'd lucked out. They were going to work construction, eventually in the motor pool of a medical headquarters at a compound being built along Highway 1. An evacuation hospital and lots of other medical outfits, all kinds of units, were to be located there. It was rumored that a jeep was traded for Whitaker and Rowe.

Trotting down the hillside toward the cluster of GP large and medium tents where he bunks and his gear waits, Whitaker is thinking, But, Sergeant Major, I already been to town. I already used my galoshes. The gravel of the pathways is cooked white from the sun, and the tents, bulky shapes darkened with dust embedded in their fibers, are peaked and scooped, like big ocean waves lit from within. Coming upon piles of uprooted tree stumps gathered in angular heaps, he slows his pace. They do not seem the remains of a tropical forest, but rather the skeletons of trees where he grew up. As sturdy and twisted as oaks or elms, they lack the curving softness of tropical growth. Roots that begin as thick as the leg of a horse end up as thin as strings six yards from their start. Taking ten or twelve tiny steps of preparation, he leaps the first of a number of holes, glimpsing crushed beer cans at the bottoms. He ducks into his tent and comes right back out with his washbasin, which he fills from one of the five-gallon cans that stand on a rack near the drainage ditch that parallels the road. The basin rests on the waist-high wall of sandbags fortifying the tents as he splashes his face. He rubs a damp towel over his belly and chest before reentering the tent for his pistol belt with ammo packs, first-aid packet, and canteen, which he shakes, checking the amount of water it contains. He slaps the belt around his hips and hooks it. He pats the right-front pocket of his trousers to be certain of his green-handled knife. He slips on a T-shirt and then a clean fatigue shirt, which he fails to button as he grabs his helmet, steel pot, and green camouflage cover, from off the hook where it hangs. Rifle slung on his shoulder, he decides to refill his canteen before setting off toward the headquarters tent, buttoning and tucking in his shirt. He walks a crooked course, wary of the tent pegs and ropes sticking up from the ground. Unable to get his shirttail arranged satisfactorily, he removes his pistol belt and loosens the blackened buckle of the belt on his trousers. The moment approaching is the part of guard he detests, a time spent in the immediate presence and under the power of the officer of the day. He runs his hands over the pockets of his uniform, making certain each button is fastened. He enters and, unsure of the extent of military procedure expected, takes up a lax position of attention. The lieutenant stands slowly from the edge of the desk on which he has been sitting while conversing with Staff Sergeant Emlin, who rests against the middle tent pole. The lieutenant is young and thin. A .45 automatic rides in a black holster strapped to his hip and tied down to his thigh by a looping thong of black leather.

Whitaker says, "Sergeant Major Wilcox sent me, sir."

"You're . . . ? " For maybe the tenth time, the lieutenant squints at the nametag above Whitaker's shirt pocket, driving home the point that Whitaker should know that he is useless and forgettable. "Whitaker."

"Yes, sir."

"First shift."

"Yes, sir."

"Let's tighten up that position of attention, soldier."

He does his best; shoves his shoulders back, heels together, the butt of his M14 steady on the floor.

Referring to a square of paper taken from the desk, the lieutenant says, "You're on at ten. It's ten to ten now." He is circling Whitaker; he taps the paper against his fingers. "What's your first general order?"

"Sir. My first general order is to take charge of this post and all government property in view."

"Inspection arms!" says the lieutenant. Whitaker raises the rifle diagonally, hooking and locking the receiver open. He offers the weapon to the lieutenant, who takes it and studies the receiver. He seems unhappy about something in the mechanism, then raises the muzzle toward the nearest lightbulb. He peers into the barrel, and they stay that way for so long Whitaker wonders who this fucking asshole thinks he's impressing. "They'll be stopping work there at ten," the lieutenant says as he returns the weapon. "Where's your flashlight?"

"It's in my tent. I'll pick it up on my way back, sir." The prolonged scrutiny provokes throbbing uneasiness.

"Come here," says the lieutenant and steps around to the back of the desk. With a pencil and a yellow pad he sketches an irregular oblong and then places about it a number of boxes and *x*s. He adds some arrows. "This is the pattern I want you to walk. These are the bunkers, the generator, et cetera. You'll have two magazines, forty rounds. But I don't want them in the weapon unless you intend to use them. While you're out there walking, you will carry your weapon empty. Only if you expect trouble—if you're sure there will be trouble—will you insert the magazine, and only if you want to kill somebody will you lock a round into a chamber."

"Yes, sir."

"That's right as rain, sir," says Sergeant Emlin. "Most a these boys in this kinda candy-ass outfit think that thing's a toy. They don't know."

"Whitaker does, though, don't you, Whitaker? You know."

"Yes, sir." He is rubbing his fingers on the sight of the rifle. Christ, he hates this fucking goddamn lieutenant.

"Here," says Seargent Emlin and Whitaker takes from him the two magazines of M14 ammunition; the weight of them pushes his hand down a little.

"Do you understand the route I want you to walk?"

"Could I take that paper with me, sir? Then I'll be sure."

"Good idea, Whitaker."

Upon stepping from the tent into the open air, he sees the men retiring from the work area, fifteen or twenty weary figures, trudging, kicking stones. He can hear the yips and scramble of a basketball game down the hill. The men coming from the bunker carry their shirts. They carry the Lyster bag. Using a shirt knotted into the shape of a ball, two of them play catch, the shirt, tumbling, the sleeves flapping. Carney is approaching Bonefezi with a couple of open beers.

"Hey, lookee the soldier," says Bonefezi, spotting Whitaker.

"Is that a soldier?"

"Sure."

"Boy oh boy."

"Pretty impressive, huh?"

"He's gonna go guard. Keep us safe."

"What you gonna guard, Whitaker?"

"The dirt," Bonefezi says.

"The bunker, too," says Whitaker.

"Very cool," someone yells.

"Sure," says Bonefezi. "We don't have somebody up there, VC gonna come in steal all our dirt. Or steal our bunker, huh. You are a serious sonofabitch of a soldier, Whitaker."

"Get fucked."

"First chance I get."

"If you was me that'd be tomorrow. Tomorrow'd be your first chance."

"Goin' to town, Whitaker. You watch out for them razor blades."

"Ho, ho, ho."

"Listen to that fucker talk that good talk," says Griffin. "Whit can talk gook, huh, Whit?"

"You mark my words," says Bonefezi. "That's some danger-ous pussy."

It is a tale often told about some Vietcong whore who, in an unexplained way, positions razor blades in her cunt, and at the arrival of an unsuspecting prick, she closes them upon it, sever-ing the prick at its root.

"You remember . . . Whitaker!" Bonefezi is hollering, hav-ing fallen several strides behind the others. Obscure in the dimness, he jumps up and down. "You come home all stumpy and bloody, you remember, ole Bonefezi warned you."

19

A gnomish man with a brown face as gouged by wrinkles as a coconut, Lan's uncle Khiem is a surprise standing in the yard of Madame Lieu's house. Though the sky is dull and overcast, he waits under a drooping palm tree. Lan approaches in a Lambretta, staring at him, her gaze intent, as if to decipher from his outer manner his most inner and secret thoughts. A nervous, feral little man, his extreme concern for triviality has always exasperated her entire family. Now he stands in the nearing dusk before the house where she works, watching her walk toward him. Eccentricity emanates from him. The odd interests of his mind affect his countenance: they seem to even change the aura of the air before him. Lan greets him respectfully and asks after the health of his sister, her mother.

"Thank you," he says, "she is well, as usual."

"What of your own wife and children?"

At this he brusquely, furiously shakes his head to show how she has irritated him. "You must join me on my motor scooter," he says. "We will go somewhere to talk."

"But I have to work."

"I spoke to grandmother here, and she does not object. Come." He turns to go. "Do you admire my motor scooter?"

"Oh, yes," she says.

Climbing the uneven slope of the roadside toward the gleam of his red-and-blue Honda, he makes demeaning remarks about the blouse and slacks she is wearing. He giggles as the insults flow across his tongue, exciting him: "The slacks are not as you think. The blouse is a stupid color. At best you look like an ignorant peasant," he says, "or a whore."

"I am a whore," she tells him.

To hear this only makes his laughter sputter into a larger, richer pleasure as he revels in the delicious privacy of some joke that is all the more precious and funny because he alone sees it.

Starting the engine, he drives off at such a slow, deliberate pace the trembling scooter barely maintains its balance. A honking jeep goes by. A dead dog lies in the road like a broken sack of garbage spilling its waste in the dirt. Big trucks rush past in both directions, some packed with crates, lumber, or laborers, others full of GIs. Pedaling toward them on the wrong side of the road a cranky bicyclist rings his bell at them. Then, beeping behind them, a Lambretta pulls out and around, its rear cab a wire mesh cage full of mournful chickens. The dusty wind teases Lan's hair into flutters.

When they have traveled what seems to her a kilometer, he veers into a tiny clearing where nameless wildflowers grow beneath barbed wire. What has he come for? she wonders. What, with his funny little mind? To stand before her dabbing dry his mouth with a white handkerchief? Her thoughts, it seems, draw from him a smirk. He removes his green-billed cap and pats his brow. Neatly he folds the handkerchief before putting it in his pocket and picking a cigarette from a tin case.

"Do you remember Phan Duy Zung?"

"Oh, yes."

"She hit her mother-in-law. It was funny to see. They argued and argued." And he shakes his head, laughing a little, as he lights his cigarette. "The mother-in-law turned to walk away. Zung hit her. Oh, yes." He sighs. "And Pham Thi Doan, who was married for two days, refused to live with her husband. Everyone told her she must go to him, but she would not. The council will decide what is to be done. They have made no decision yet, but it will be to let her do as she wishes, I am sure. Or she will do as she wishes anyway. The people are all very strange today. More and more. Nguyen Van Ly got into an argument with Le Van Doc and nearly killed him hitting him with a hammer. I suspected such things were possible from Ly. Indeed." His fraught little giggle is a steady counterchord beneath each word and intricate sentence, a fuzzy, happy breathing that increases in amazement at each story's ending. In the barbershop he runs in their home village, he gathers gossip like a bird collecting the makings of a nest. He snips and cuts away, and the hair of people's heads settles to his floor, as do the stories of his customers. He rests his odd brain in a home built of the curious events of their daily lives. Now he breathes to a slower rhythm. Softer, the sound has less frenzy in it. "I am here, Lan," he says, "to get a picture of you. Your mother has no pictures of you. I searched all through your house. Searched and searched."

"A photograph?" she says. "Of me?"

"Yes, yes; there are none, your mother says with so many moves and the terrible fire. Only those already on the altar were rescued. If you don't have any, you must get one prepared and give it to me. I will come back when it's ready. Can you do that? Lan, I have worried about our family—you have no father, and you can die so far away from home as you are."

"I don't understand," she says.

"Ahhhhhhhhhhhhhh," he says, his voice husky with the intimation of something known by him to be grander and different than what she means. "Nor do I. But I have pictures of myself safely in my home; my wife keeps them. Your mother keeps pictures of me. My younger brother. I will be represented and remembered. But you—perhaps strangers will bury you. What if they do and they forget about you? You would not be represented on the altar. You are young; you don't worry about such things. More and more each day is neglected, but I will not join this failure, this indifference. The bird goes to his nest, and we go to our family. The altars in the homes of the Vietnamese people have today more pictures than people to pray before them. We die and die." His breath grows shaky and thin, until a spasm lifts it into laughter. "I'm late," he says, looking at his watch. "I must go to Saigon. Do you not want a place upon the communal altar? You wander so alone and miserable now. It will only be worse when you are dead. Next week. One week from today. Bring the photo to work and I will meet you."

"All right," she says.

"Did I tell you Quach Thi Ba was going to remarry? You remember her husband, Huy, was killed not even three years ago in the terrible fighting at Bac Tin. His body was not found.

Many were buried in big graves. All together, both sides. Lost and dead. Or given no burial at all, but left to be eaten by the animals. His ghost came to her house. His spirit voice shouted in the dark at her. He looked cold and wet and hungry, Ba said. She told everyone. He was bitter and frantic; she could not marry, she was his wife. He was lost and wandering but he was coming back to her. He was going to live again. He loved her still and she must wait. He begged her to remember him, to honor him." Her uncle's dark eyes were as shiny as beetle shells. "Do you like Ba? What do you think of her?"

"I like her. But she always thought I was too young and silly to be her friend."

"I never liked her. But I will have pity on her. She came to me for help in building a Windy Tomb for Huy. And to write a poem inviting him to rest in the empty place waiting to be his home." His face pulls tighter, making his mouth seem a gash about to widen by tearing his cheeks. "So many ghosts." He sighs. His shrug is followed by his odd little laugh. "You know, of course, it was always my thought to have a book of genealogy as complete and accurate as the Duc family. That would be such a wonderful possession. But it will not ever be, now. What am I to do? People die and they are born but no one notifies me. We are all over the country. I have seen the Duc family book. It is so accurate. What envy I feel. All deceased family names and the dates of birth and of death, all filial relationships. Everything. It is such a wonderful thing. But even they are having trouble, even with all their money. How can we keep track of it all? Who can do it? Everyone is so scattered. All families are scattered. I have two brothers in the north. What do we know of them? I told your father it was a mistake to leave, mixed in with all those Catholics. I knew we were wrong. He said the land would be better to the south. The Communists all kept warning that the Americans would lie to us; they would take us far out to sea and drown us. We would never reach the south, the Communists told us. And the Catholics did nothing but talk with their priests about their Holy Virgin who had gone to sea and they must follow. In the middle were we. Doing what? Going south."

"I have a photograph at my home, Uncle. I have one," she tells him.

"Taken for this purpose. It must be taken for the purpose of which I have spoken."

"It was."

"It must be serious."

"Yes."

"You are lying."

"No."

"Can we go get it now?"

"I should work, Uncle. I can't leave."

"Tomorrow then." He looks at his watch. "I must see your brother in Saigon and after him my own second son, Thuy. I will come in the afternoon."

"Thuy is not at home?"

"No. Come."

She feels it happen to her as he walks away, the dark spirit dragging her off from life. She looks to the nearest house and sees an oil lamp lit on a table, and then shadows in the deepening dusk. Would she be like Huy, wandering between the two worlds, homeless and forgotten?

Her uncle sighs as the Honda chugs along the gray concrete, stained brown and red with dust in the lowering evening. She hugs his waist, and while examining her many memories of him all colored by her bitter past dislike, she feels a new and tender gratitude toward his funny little mind that has thought to care for her. She squeezes his skinny waist and bumps her brow against his shoulder.

"Stop," he scolds. "I am not one of your customers."

The photo she wants to give him shows her in a lovely *Ao Dais,* the tunic and panels a rich purple, she knows, though merely black and white in the picture, the pantaloons a lesser shade. As if tall and regal, she gazes off to the side of the frame with a slight expression of pleasure and of calm. In her fingers is an orchid. Around her stand vases in a balanced arrangement, each with a wildflower that enhances the orchid she holds. She is a vase amid many vases, all containing flowers. The floor, washed in varied light, seems a watery pond in places, while looking as rugged as stone elsewhere.

This is the photo that will hold her on the altar, she thinks, in her surprisingly celebratory mind, and upon her dying, candlesticks, and incense, flowers, and jars of rice alcohol will surround her, while in a nearby tabernacle reside four generations of the names of her ancestors. Those to whom she is unknown will know her only as she appears in the photo. On her anniversary, prayers will be offered along with food, and burning items, such as paper shoes, clothing, and money, all that she might need, living in the other world.

"Remember," her uncle says as she stands before him in the yard of Madame Lieu's house, "the French and the Viet Minh and the girls who were whores to the French—how they were forgiven and cared for by the Viet Minh, given education and new lives. But those who loved and married Frenchmen and were their wives, or loved and lived with them as concubines— remember how they were disemboweled, their stomachs cut out, the rest of them left to linger a little and think of their losses." An odd and magical light burns in his eyes, hints of laughter and joy that please him deeply, as he makes one last remark before driving off down the street into early evening: "You remember, Niece, how there is a future."

"Yes," she says, turning to encounter Sa, Madame Lieu's infant niece, waddling about bemused and hiccuping. Lan dances to grab the girl and lift her upward toward the sky. They are leaves, she thinks, and they are branches, she and Sa, continuing each other, the way Lan's own children will one day continue her, remembering her father and grandfather and uncle. Lan is happy, and she loves the child who has given her this pleasure of spinning below a beautiful, multicolored sky twirling beyond the child's giddy, enraptured face. Lan loves Sa, who compels her to lift and spin. Does not Sa, with her presence, spin them both and give this happiness?

20

There was a guy in Whitaker's high school like Bonefezi. Because Whitaker trekked in from the country to high school in nearby Platteville, he knew a variety of kids, both farm kids and Platteville kids. Walking toward the area he is assigned to guard, he thinks about going to school in his father's truck, and then he thinks about his father lying motionless under all those covers in that big bed in Wisconsin at this very instant. It doesn't make any sense, so damn hot here and still winter there. His father had big callused hands and was maybe too quick to fly off the handle, but if he said he'd be there, he showed up. Whitaker traveled to grade school by bus, but his father drove him and Roger three miles to the pickup spot each day. Later on when Roger was in high school and had a car of his own, he drove Whitaker to the bus stop. Then Whitaker started high school, and Roger drove them both all the way to school and back. But Roger graduated when Whitaker was about to become a sophomore, so the job fell to his father. In good weather, the trip took maybe forty minutes, which meant his dad had to waste the same amount of time getting back to the farm. Whenever he could, Whitaker bummed a ride home. But often the best he could arrange was to get dropped off at the house of a friend who lived along the way. And then one winter morning, with the both of them finishing up pancakes and gulping coffee before rushing out to the truck, Whitaker realized he was in a brand-new, special kind of companionship with his father. He hadn't ever really thought of such a thing. They were alone a lot, Roger having gone off to work at a car dealership owned by a friend's older brother. Whitaker started trying to think of things he might say to his father, or maybe even some questions he might ask. He wondered what he wanted to know. Then winter came and he watched his father face down blinding sleet and long, ice-disguised stretches of pavement. When the old F100 Dually struggled and fishtailed, his dad cursed, demanding that the tires with their goddamn overpriced chains catch. If the windshield froze up so it looked like they were trying to see through paraffin, he poked his head out the open side window. Occasionally, they spun to a halt. Even though Whitaker was sixteen and strong, he was told to get behind the wheel while his father went out and manhandled the truck, shouting and shoving until the damn thing got back where it belonged and acted like it was supposed to.

It was in the late spring that one Saturday his father pulled the Nash into the yard with Roger following in the truck. His dad had made the purchase at the lot where Roger worked. Two mornings later, as Whitaker drove off on his own for the first time, he had such a sense of negligence, he was sure he'd forgotten something. He braked and looked in the rearview mirror, and he saw his father by the front door laughing, and he laughed, too. They were both free now, and then he looked again. The old man was turning away, walking into the house. The door closed and the empty front porch looked abandoned and forlorn and forgotten when that wasn't the case at all.

Whitaker, following, as best he can, the lieutenant's stupid map, goes along the road. It's annoying to have these stupid directions; he's pulled guard before without them, but he feels like he better try to do as they say. It looks like he should turn at the ditch and go toward the area behind the bunker. The ground is a dusty pale brown under the moon. It's pocked with holes and strewn with stones that seesaw under his boots. The coiled concertina wire has a leaden color as he arrives beside it, though the many barbs to his left and right, hit with moonlight, seem silverish. He strolls for a time along the wire before halting to look down toward the Vung Tau highway and the ammo dump. Nothing moves and there is no sound but a barking dog far off and then another dog closer picking up the cry. He loosens the sling on his rifle and switches it to his left shoulder, then checks the map and walks toward the bunker. My first general order, he thinks, is to take charge of this post and all government property in view. My second general order is to walk my post in a military manner, keeping always on the alert and observing everything that takes place within sight or hearing. Fuck me, he thinks. I guess that means I can't whack off.

The barking has ceased; he's back on the road. The road vanishes to his left at a hill. The guy like Bonefezi in Whitaker's high school was a Platteville kid named Silvestri. Silvestri and Whitaker and all of them hated school, and Mr. Prendergast, the chemistry teacher, was weak, a regular milquetoast, and they all knew it the minute they saw him, so he was their goat. Once they hung fifty Trojan prophylactics all over the classroom; they hung them from the lights and from the radiators, they taped them to the blackboard. Mr. Prendergast, arriving as the bell rang, tried to pretend he hadn't noticed by proceeding directly into his lecture, until Silvestri raised his hand. Ignored for several minutes, Silvestri climbed up onto his desk and after several more minutes, began stomping his feet until Mr. Prendergast looked at him and he cried out, Sir, what's the point? There are dirty goddamn prophylactic rubbers hanging all over our classroom, Mr. Prendergast. Dirty goddamn prophylactic sexual rubbers! What's the point?

Whitaker is back at the wire and again the cries of the dogs have begun. That was a good thing ole Silvestri and me did, he thinks, seeing himself somehow at the center of the story. Then the sudden, hollow *whoom-whoom* of two mortar rounds firing startles him, and he flinches but hears no trace of their trajectory until there is a faint and distant double thudding where they hit. He wonders, should he perhaps insert a magazine, knowing, of course, he shouldn't, but still, maybe he might prepare himself a little. He will lock the receiver open; he will unfasten the catch of one ammo pack. But then he worries that walking around with the receiver open could get dirt in it. Should some of the enemy actually come, how would he behave? Kill the fuckers, he thinks. Bang, bang. He is at the road, peering over lengths of desolate terrain featureless in the dark except for patches of gravel catching light from somewhere, and empty except for the hulking machinery, stacks of tools, the mound of dirt near the ragged outlines of the half-built bunker. Silence has returned. They did a lot of funny stuff to Mr. Prendergast. He is walking again, taking long steps controlled by a slow, methodical inner rhythm. In this manner he negotiates the whole area, thinking only of his walking until he finds that tiny, quick steps seem more interesting. Though he intends to walk the entire route in this new, entertaining style, he suddenly quits. He's at the very edge of the compound. He's at the perimeter. There has been no firing for a while now. Deciding he will sit for a little on a stack of empty sandbags, he puts the rifle to his shoulder to aim into the dark. Bang, bang, dead gook; bang, bang. And one time Silvestri took the anatomy skeleton out of its jarlike case, and after hiding it, he climbed into the jar himself, so he was standing there looking out grinning when Mr. Prendergast entered the room. Get out of there, Silvestri, yelled Mr. Prendergast. Get out of there right this minute. Where's the skeleton? Silvestri only smiled. Whitaker is grinning. Mr. Prendergast tried to force open the door of the jar, which worked like a coffin lid, but Silvestri held it shut from the inside. Mr. Prendergast screamed, You get out of there right this minute, Silvestri! I mean it now—where is the skeleton? That skeleton is worth a lot of money. Money! screamed Silvestri and burst out of the case to run around the room opening cabinets, slamming doors and drawers. Everyone, all of them joined in. It's not here, Mr. Prendergast! Not here! Slam! Bang! Not in your desk, Mr. Prendergast. Bang! Slam! Not here! Not here! Where did you last see it!

A flare appears, so distant it seems a star. He stops at the sight of it hanging miles out among the ghostly hills. There is fighting in the jungle there, a skirmish. Another flare, a spark creasing the total black, leaps up and then another comes. Three match flames in the enormity of that black sky. He grows tense, listening, tilted toward those trembling, airborne specks to hear the gunfire. He waits, straining, but no sound comes and then the grinding rumble of a truck reaches him, faintly, gearing down for power, and he sees it moving with its headlights off way down below where the evac hospital has a few lights on. And then something else happens: a shout. A light comes on much closer, the beam darting crazily. It's a flashlight. Someone is running on the paths among the tents where Whitaker lives and they're waving a flashlight all over the place and they're yelling, but Whitaker can't make any sense of what they're saying. Other lights pop on in scattered tents and then more and more lights, and people are coming out from some of the tents. Whitaker jams a magazine into his rifle. He locks and loads a round; he pushes the safety on. Something is wrong. He sets off at a trot. Guys are zigzagging around. Most of them wear T-shirts and underwear. They run and yell and some start beating on metal, their canteen cups or something. "Snake! Snake! Big fucking snake!"

"Where? Where?" Whitaker calls; he's the only one armed.

"Griffin went down to take a shit, and there was this big fucking snake. Twenty feet long at least. Thirty. Forty." It's Doland standing there in his fatigue cap, Bermuda shorts, and flip-flops.

The floodlights at the basketball court go on, and Whitaker thinks he sees a flash on the gravel, a bolt of whipping dull gray that seems to have no end and then it's gone. "Did you see that?"

"What?"

"It was right there, Doland. Do you think I should shoot it?"

"What? Where?"

Down near the latrine there's an excited cry. It's a bunch of people yelling all at once in a kind of swelling cheer, like at a football game. Several guys run past Whitaker into the tents, and other guys run in the opposite direction. One of them is carrying an armload of beer, and he goes backward for a few steps so he can announce, "Randall says the stupid thing went into the shit trench. It's in the shit trench. They saw it. Fucking thing's a monster."

Now Whitaker is positive he saw it; that's what it was on the basketball court, he's sure of it. Still, he wants a better look.

"Whitaker! What the hell are you doing? Stop where you are."

It's the lieutenant coming straight at him, and he's got his pants on, his boots, too, his baseball cap with its bar and a T-shirt. "What the hell are you doing?"

"I saw all the hullabaloo, sir, and there's a big snake, so—"

"What's your fifth general order?"

"What?"

"Tell me your fifth general order, Whitaker! I want you to tell me your fifth general order."

"I saw all the noise and everybody and I—"

"What did I just ask you?"

"My fifth, sir?"

"To quit my post only when properly relieved," the lieutenant barks at him. "That's your fifth general order! Do you want to end up in the stockade?"

"What?"

"What's your fifth general order? You spit it out!"

"To quit my post only when properly relieved! Sir!"

"Is this your post?"

"What?"

"Have you been properly relieved?"

"No, sir."

"And is this your post? Right here?"

"No, sir."

"So where is it? Where is your post?"

Whitaker takes off toward the bunker, striding briskly and then breaking into a trot. The gigantic slapping sound, the whoosh and the yellow wall of light that balloons over him and throws his shadow down onto the dirt ahead, like a ghost squirming in the gravel, turns him around. Fire is reaching from the latrine area where he knows the latrine box can be moved off the shit trench so the shit can be burned. The way everybody's hooting and carrying on, they must have moved the box, poured in gasoline and diesel, and then ignited the trench with the snake still in it. They're burning the shit with the snake in it. The flames rocket and rattle. The stink of burning fuel, the stench of the shit, and the heat roll over him. The whole campsite is vivid and weird, like it's going to blink out and be gone. Then shouting starts up again. It had been silenced or covered by the fire. But he doesn't dare look any longer, because even though the lieutenant has been caught up by the spectacle, Whitaker knows the prick will wheel around and glare at him any second now.

He hurries on to the bunker, and once he's there, he ducks behind it. He sits down in the dirt with his rifle resting on his lap. What a crazy thing. That snake was dinky dow. Why would it just do that, just crawl into their camp? The way it was running, it was scared of people. He feels like he saw its eyes, even though he couldn't have. He hates snakes. He's killed them all his life. Every time he saw one all over Wisconsin. So why does he feel sort of bad? Did he really see its eyes? Even though he couldn't have. Maybe it was trying to get the garbage. Maybe it was hungry. Or maybe it used to live here. In the jungle that used to be here. He stands quickly and looks around warily. Did he have to worry about that now? Because if it lived here, others might have lived here, too. The snake might have brothers and sisters. It might have come looking for them. They might be looking for him. They might all come back.

The fire has died down and the campsite is quiet. A couple of men stand talking. They look like officers, but he can't really tell. He turns once more toward the hills that seem empty now, silent and dark. In the daylight a village is often discernible in that area, tin roofs and a church steeple shimmering in the sun like scattered toy blocks. But there's just the darkness. Full of secrets. Two flares climb from the black, and then tracer rounds float up from one point and sink in another. The first of the flares sputters and goes out, while the other, with a slight lateral drift, descends. But up leaps a new one to make a pair, then a third and a fourth climb to form a cone of leaden whiteness. A nearer noise whirls him around, beginning to aim the rifle. A figure is crossing the field toward him. Reese. It's midnight—past midnight, actually. Reese is late. Whitaker's shift is over.

And the way he feels, it's like someone out there beneath those failing flares is dying now. He has heard nothing, seen nothing, but someone is dead, having put up light to find the enemy all around him. Alert to the silence in which there is only the scrape and grind of Reese approaching, his mind has eyes to see into that blackness and then even further, into another day when someone on one of those hills will look over the miles from there to here—to this place where Whitaker will be standing, having desperately sent up flares in a call for help as the enemy closes in on him. Poor fucking Mr. Prendergast, he thinks. He can hear the steps of Reese behind him getting nearer. One afternoon as Mr. Prendergast entered, the entire class bellowed in unison, Good morning, Mr. Hoosier! He glanced at them, only the briefest alarm in his eyes as he sat down behind his desk. They called, How are you this morning, Mr. Hoosier? I'm not Mr. Hoosier, he said. Yes, you are. I'm Mr. Prendergast. No, Mr. Hoosier, don't you know your name? I'm Mr. Prendergast! No! We're tired of calling you Prendergast. Prendergast is stupid.

Reese arrives and Whitaker hands over the forty rounds of ammunition that they are not to put into their rifles unless they mean to kill somebody. Reese says he would like to get a shot at a VC as long he was old and coming in backwards.

"Did you see the snake?"

"No. I was tryin' to sleep, man. You can guess how screwed up that was. The place was a loony bin. Did you see it?"

Whitaker shakes his head, and hands over the lieutenant's map and Reese stares at it. "What the fuck is this?"

"It's the route we're supposed to walk."

"Who says?"

"The lieutenant drew it up."

"You're puttin' me on."

"No."

"You gotta be kiddin' me."

"No." The flares have vanished. The sky and landscape look peaceful. The heart attack that felled Whitaker's father landed with the force of a truck. He yelped and shoved out with his fist, as if to fend off a thing he could see, all the while going down like a man bowing, only he didn't stop. Whitaker had been about to walk from the kitchen and he turned back at the yell, and before he knew to kneel down, before he knew to telephone for help, he stood there, frozen.

Reese points at the diagram and says, "What's this?"

Whitaker looks. "The bunker."

"No kidding."

He leaves Reese muttering and turning the map upside down and around, every which way. "This is fucked up, man," he says. Whitaker staggers a little, actually stepping sideways to catch his balance. Soon he will sleep. A little further along in the night, he will be awakened to walk some more. At six AM, he will go to work. And like a filament in his mind, without which he could not see anything at all, there begin to hover and glow the tiny dark-haired bodies of the girls in the countryside and villages who everyone says are riddled with sickness beneath their loveliness. But he doesn't care. What can he care? In the afternoon he will go and move within and against them. Find a part no one has taken time to find. Make her breathe. See the changes in her eyes. Hear her.

21

Whitaker stands with the Lambretta driver watching the black soldier punch the girl. What was her name? Lan. The blow comes straight out from the shoulder. The heel of the hand, fingers raised, palm forward, splats against her cheek, and she shrieks, sobbing, but unable to flee because his other hand clenches her arm. She wears dark blue slacks, a lighter blue blouse. Her shirt-tail has come loose and it shivers over her hips as he hits her again. His voice is shrill with fury. Whitaker can't understand a word he's saying, and she's squealing in Vietnamese. Her pawing hands work the air, as if to find a way to escape. Her voice and manner are stricken and innocent; he has no right to hit her.

Confused about what to do, Whitaker grimaces at the wide-eyed, grinning Lambretta driver beside him. "What does she say?"

"Eeuuhhhh!" the man laughs, his flashing eyes aflutter. "Talk numba ten. Ohhh." He shakes his head, claps his hands while Whitaker looks back and is taken by the urge to dash up and throw this asshole off her. Still, he squelches the impulse, wary of his own hair-trigger temper, his sides and chest wet with sweat. A fight could mean trouble, the stockade, or worse, because this guy's in civvies and sunglasses, so there's no way to be sure he isn't 1st Division or 173rd or the 25th, some crazed grunt in from the field where he'd spent last week in the shit in some paddy killing people. Awareness of how little he knows about the girl's life is a hole into which his desire to move keeps falling, as she stomps her feet and pulls free somehow of the black soldier's grip. Would she even remember Whitaker? Isn't it only his grandly babbling self-conceit that believes she might? Before him, the two of them glare out of feelings and histories he knows nothing about, and little in their behavior reveals anything but anger. This guy could be her boyfriend. The fury between them could come from months or more of bed and screwing, gifts, all kinds of shit. Or if they're strangers, she could have robbed him, cheated somehow. What does Whitaker know other than how he is here, looking at them? His ignorance is too much, a burden he cannot budge, though it hurts a little to witness her pain. Then the black guy, eyes still raving, is leaving, knocking aside a parked bicycle, and Whitaker, watching, a little drunk and sad, suddenly panics that Lan will see him standing there, having done nothing. Should he do something? What? In this confusion, the alternatives of going forward to her, or just staying where he is, appear equally impossible, so he turns sideways and goes jogging off, head bowed over the worn, dusty pathway, the feeble grass. Along this road are many bars

where there will be booze and some other girl to screw. Upon
him descends, as he runs, a ghost of the scorn that could have
befallen him, and deservedly, too, if he'd actually gotten into a
fight over some gook whore he scarcely knows. He feels relief
at having escaped such a mistake, and can't understand why
he came so close. Maybe he would have been better off staying
at the compound and sleeping instead of rushing into town.
Finished with guard he could have fallen into bed rather than
wandering over to help Rowe put up framing for the officer's
billet, a choice that entitled him to be off duty at lunchtime.
He grabbed a quick meal washed down with a ton of coffee,
finally managed his long-delayed shower, and after throwing
on civilian clothes, *di di*-the-fuck-*mau*ed out of there, arriving
in Tan Mai across the street from the car wash just in time to
see her get punched in the face.

The sun is burning, boiling waves; it hammers at him; it
cooks stiffness into the back of his neck, and he slows down,
trudging along, peeping into this bar and that one. He sees dirt
floors and tile floors. Over and over there are shelves of booze
behind wooden bar-tops or tinted bar-tops edged in aluminum
strips, a jumble of lovelorn music and tiresome GIs, until finally, he parts a beaded curtain and pushes from the heat into
dimness, a blue wicker chair and table, where he flops down,
for whatever reason done for the day. The music in this lurid
place is tinny and cheery and of all things—*Lollipop*—that stupid song from high school. Lollipop, lollipop. Catchy as hell,
but he doesn't care. It hurts so bad, he's feeling so sad. The girl
who brings his beer is thin and long legged. His dissatisfaction,
he believes, comes from nothing. It's just the way it is. Just who
he is. That's all. A reasonless, sourceless case of being Whitaker in a foul mood. The plain wood floor is covered here and

there by rugs, and the mamasan, who comes up and smiles and says, "You want nice girl?" is creepy. Younger than most, she has flat, killer eyes. Probably a whore who worked her way up, salvaging nickels and dimes, until she got to be boss. Now the money runs to her from the others. He imagines the funnel-like process of her business: her hands wait at her girl's asses for the money they shit, coming in their snatches.

Tall brown bottles of Bommniba Beer 33 drained empty except for plumes of shadow collect on the table before him. When he goes into the backyard to pee, the long-legged girl follows, so he gets a good look at her. She eyes him and goes back inside. A bunch of kids are squatted nearby gambling. Dice and money fly about a large sheet of paper spread over a flat rock and covered with drawings of a deer, a fish, a chicken, and maybe a crab. All boys, a shambles of scrawny legs sticking out of tattered shorts, they yammer and babble as more money gets scattered. Then some kid throws the dice, and they all scream and shout and poke each other.

When a little later he finishes screwing the long-legged girl, she holds up the sagging rubber. "You see, GI," she says. "Numba one." It's proof of the deed, as if he didn't know.

Early evening has subdued the hot colors of the road and the searing sky seems to have relented, becoming a lesser, cooler blue. A group of galloping boys all but knock over a young girl carrying a laundry bag, a gurgling infant on her hip. The girl yelps and calls after them in a scolding tone. She's dressed in a white blouse and black pajama bottoms and looks about twelve, red flip-flops on her bare feet. When one of the boys stops to scoop up a stone, which he hurls back at her, she ducks protectively over the baby. Whitaker takes several threatening steps toward the gang, and they flee. The girl doesn't notice and he watches her drop the laundry bag, flip her conical straw hat forward to take it off and fan the baby and herself. She looks weary and demoralized, and yet as she starts back up, she has a bounce in her step and she's smiling and talking to the baby. His own mood is curiously soft. He feels beaten, useless and forgotten, just like the lieutenant made sure he felt last night, like the army wants him twenty-four hours a day. He feels like there's something he should do. If only he could start working in the motor pool like he's supposed to. He hasn't slept in hours. Going back to the compound and hitting his rack for some rest would be the smart thing, and he knows it, yet he does nothing to make it happen, doesn't even look down the road for a Lambretta to transport him. He just keeps walking, wandering to no purpose he understands beyond the inexact urgings, the moods and half moods that stoke the pointless engine of this aimless afternoon. Off to his right, a bridge spans a black slice of water. Widening, the dull surface harbors a row of bamboo shanties that extend out over the gray stillness on stilts.

Two tiger-striped South Vietnamese soldiers, small and wiry, babble to each other beside the gateposts of a house until they turn to him as he passes. "Hey, GI," says one. "You want girl? Numba one girl. You want numba one girl? I no have. No have numba one."

"No sweat," Whitaker says.

"Got numba fuckin' ten. Got boucoup numba fuckin' ten girl. You want? Got clap. Got VD. Boucoup. Got boucoup sick girl. You want? Got numba ten. Numba ten thou. GI. Hey, you want talk me you want numba fuckin' ten thou sick girl?"

The face and voice are laughing in a pointless attempt to mask the ARVN's pathetic, loopy desperation that makes Whitaker nod a little, chuckle, but otherwise maintain his silence. He has his own troubles. Something in this day has made him begin to worry about the progress of his life. It feels lost. He has no time for these men. His own life is nowhere he can see; it's absent from this road, absent from the damp, unpleasant odors of rot and fish and manure, the oppressive, never-ending heat. If only they'd let him work where he's supposed to so he could at least get his hands on a carburetor, a transmission, a drive shaft. All night he walked in circles to protect junk and in the morning there was nowhere to go for a decent breakfast. You can be shot any instant and everybody is crazy. He wants a malted milk, a Dairy Queen with a blond carhop; he wants people making dates and plans for fun and movies. A vision of himself couched in a red Ferrari comes and goes achingly through him; his fingers twitch with his dream of downshifting on spraying gravel, the huge engine popping with deceleration to announce his return to the Dairy Queen.

Blinking up from this image, he sees a dead dog kicked to the side of the road where it lies in the colorful mess of its guts. And was there anything in his life to indicate that he was moving toward the possibility of ever realizing the dream he'd just had? No. There was nothing. And what could he point to in his past that might have started him in the right direction? Same answer. He's like a dull lead ball in a pinball machine bouncing from flipper to flipper to pillar to pillar to wall to hole, lighting up little, scoring nothing. Zilch. He feels bad. Bad about who he is, where he is, what he's done. Bad about everything. Is that the reason—his aimlessness? Maybe he doesn't know the reason, but he knows how he feels. The sudden tugging on his shirt turns out to be a little girl with white scars like worms on both cheeks. She's tattered from head to toe and clings to his shirttail and holds out her hand, doing her best to say, "Gimme money, GI." Whitaker hands over a hundred Ps. The kid keeps flapping her fingers at him for more. Maybe now in the desolation of this fucked-up country, amid these poor miserable empty people, he will be able to find himself, he thinks, somehow locating the lost part of himself that he knows is in there, the secret Whitaker who wants to help him fulfill his needs and duties, so that he gets what he wants. He gives another hundred Ps to the girl and fifty more and vows that upon returning to the States, he will make use of his opportunities from now on. He will arrive on time for his job. No hour will be too early, no task will be seen as beneath him. He will whip his lazy brain into shape so it knows about more than engines, V8s or 6s, more than timing, sequence, and firing, but the business end, too, the social skills necessary to run a garage. He will become expert at customer relations. Yes, oh yes, oh boy yes. The way to the speed of that Ferrari and everything else he wants in life is gotten through the drudgery of straightforward labor. He knows about work. He's not afraid of work. He just has to put his mind to it, apply himself, and he can own his own garage where others perform for him whatever task he tells them to. No need to feel down. He's nowhere near his last chance to make something of himself. The real possibilities of his life can't be found here and now in this moment in this place. But he's not doomed to stay. He won't be here forever. This isn't his natural stomping ground. It doesn't matter what happens here. It's hardly even real life.

With his feet at intersecting pathways, he sees his dusty civilian shoes, and they seem far from home, and he stares, telling himself this is where he is, right here, right now; and he's thirsty. He turns sharply in the hope of a beer with which to celebrate his decision to change his life, and in the deepening twilight he encounters Lan, framed in a window, watching him, a strangely lavender silhouette in a lavender dress.

"Hello," he says.

"Hello, you-you."

He nearly walks away, instantly embarrassed. He struggles, his mind racing as he searches her expression to determine if she knows he stood by while that black soldier punched her out. The thought, the search, reawakens his guilt. He notes how this house with its faded orange stucco walls is not a part of the car wash, though it's in the same neighborhood. She looks away from him. Is she pouting? Sadness tinges the air about her and he feels it drag at him, a call for sympathy that makes him resentful. But then her sulky invitation flowers into something hopeful, as he sees her desire for sympathy rather than guilt as proof that she knows nothing about his failure to help her. Though she scarcely lifts her head to look at him, he believes she wants him to stay. She appears pretty again, very pretty, much prettier than before. Scents of perfume and powder enhance the air. Makeup highlights her eyes, her funny cheeks. Her dress, lavender, with a pattern of flowers embroidered at the waist and breast, is clean and neatly pressed. He's glad to see her.

"Hello, hello," he says.

"For sure."

"How you-you, Lan?"

"Okay."

"Good."

"You dinky dow?"

"Tee-tee," he says and adds, "Boucoup sleepy," meaning himself, moving closer, gesturing vaguely.

"No," she says. "Me numba one. No sleepy."

"No. Me," he says, pointing to his chest. "Me sleepy. Me tee-tee dinky dow, boucoup sleepy."

"You go Bien Hoa," she says. "Do fuck-fuck bar girl. I know. Numba one."

"Oh, never happen."

"Bien Hoa numba one girl."

"No," he says. "No."

"*Sou,* I know. No sweat."

"No lie. Do many beer. No girl."

"Okay. No sweat."

"No sweat," he says.

It seems they've agreed about something, and he wonders what it is. Her mood continues to affect him, like a circle of warmth into which he has stepped, a kind of spell drawing him closer. As if on her breath, her sadness comes into the air and he takes it in. He leans against the wall, peering in the window. There's a candle on a little table and a book lies beside it. A small white envelope lies on top of the book. He studies her closely, but sees no evidence of where that jerkoff hit her, though she probably covered it with makeup. Now she is preparing to speak, her eyes seeking to measure if he cares at all. The lids narrow, the head bows to warn him that she expects denial, that she awaits defeat. But there is petition in her upward glance; she flirts. "You buy me orange, Whitaker?"

"Ohhhhh," he says, and shakes his head. This is not what he wants. "Must go compound."

"Buy me one orange."

It's late; he's tired. "Must go compound," he tells her.

"Tee-tee. We go my house. I do prick you."

The complete absence in him of any interest in getting laid is so amazing, momentarily, that it makes him stare and think.

She pouts. And then it seems that going to the compound is a kind of spell, too, only weaker than the one cast by her nearness, no more than a vague urge that is evaporating and leaving him there. He'll do a good deed, she feels so bad. "Okay," he says. "One orange." She springs to her feet and comes out the door.

The stall toward which she guides him is in front of a shanty with a ragged canopy shading three closely arranged tables and chairs. It's located near the road but below a shoulder so steep it has the appearance of a ditch. Lan keeps looking at him with an unnervingly happy expression and Whitaker, walking, has the sensation that by letting her hold his hand this way he's being hauled into a realm outside the rule most GIs adhere to, which is that you give nothing but your hard-on and your money to these whores. It's not a distinction that he likes or wants. Anxiety stirs as they enter under the shadowy roof, and he wonders at her power to pull him here. With grand gestures and eyes full of pride, she orders a Coke for him, an orange for herself, and then snuggles onto his lap for all the world of rumbling trucks, jeeps, and buzzing scooters to gawk at. In his gut there rolls a wave of resentment, and he wishes the dark would hurry up.

Plunging within inches of the edge of the steep shoulder, a jeep clanks to a halt, sending up dust and pebbles. The brawny lieutenant who springs from behind the wheel wears the lightning-bolt patch of the 25th Infantry Division. In clipped, hard tones he speaks to Lan of someone, a girl, Whitaker guesses, a name that sounds like Cam the way he says it. Lan explains that Cam has gone away. Lan doesn't know where, but, "Cam say to say him her love. Cam boucoup love him." The lieutenant says he'll come back tomorrow. "For sure," says

Lan. When the man's eyes pass over Whitaker plopped there with his whore on his lap, they have a fierce and cool hate.

She is playing with his ear. Her pressing body increases the already stifling heat, making his sweat pour. A kind of fear, nameless and taunting, is loose in him. When a chugging Lambretta goes by with a couple of GIs aboard, he thinks they smirk at him, and then the proprietor of the stall lowers the canopy and chatters at Lan, who makes it clear they should move inside. Hardly have the drinks arrived when Whitaker has to rise and go pee. He staggers out the back considering clandestine flight. But thoughts of her sad face, his power to change it just by saying he would buy her an orange drink hold him. His nagging inability to forget how he did nothing while standing by and watching a man beat her pulls at him to go back. His guilt is a hole through which she can reach him at any time, and she doesn't even know it's there. It's laughable. And now two drunken Vietnamese soldiers stand on either side of her as he returns. Coming around the corner, he stops. She sits at one of the little tables shifted inside. The edge of the wall against which his hand is pressed has a weatherworn, splintering surface. His immediate confusion brings on tension that flows into his fingers and turns them rigid. With care, he starts across the space of ground between himself and them, thinking he will check and double-check the situation. They are after this girl he wants to be rid of. So what is this slow, steady grind of anger that has begun to claim him? Another American soldier is there. In the gray air, a freckle-faced kid lounges on his side on a bench, his fingers tapping the top of his beer. Whitaker can't recall seeing him before, and he notices, also, the strangeness of how there has been no response yet to his arrival. The owner lights an oil lamp, and the flickering reveals the tiger-striped ARVNs as the pair who jeered at him earlier. Lan's brief happiness is gone. She looks downcast and sullen, her gaze on the floor. The men, in their camouflage fatigues splotched with variations of green and black, have jungle hats hanging on their backs from strings around their throats; they babble and poke at her. He tries to see if they have weapons and wonders whether the lumps in their baggy trousers are grenades, but there's no way to tell.

Near enough now to perceive in the dimness the other American's gaze, he frowns at what he thinks is sneering amusement, and halts, suddenly reluctant to go any closer. Faltering here, he is spotted by one of the ARVNs; the tawny face grins, like a light going on. The man yelps to his friend and points at Whitaker.

"Hello," says the one who spotted him. "GI, hey, you see. I talk you numba fuckin' ten girl." He points at Lan. "Okay, numba fuckin' ten thou, you see?"

"What's goin' on?" says Whitaker.

"Here's the deal," drawls the other GI. "They feel like she oughtta go back of the shed with 'em. You know. Suck 'em off; give 'em blow jobs, screw 'em, whatever, and she's bein' coy, like she don't know what they're sayin'."

Halfway through this languid explanation, Whitaker has become aware of the intense focus of Lan's eyes upon him. "You understand gook talk?" he says to the GI.

"Hey, Whitaker," she says.

"I got me an ear for languages, shit."

At the call of Whitaker's name, the farthest Vietnamese bends close to her, his voice humming. Now she shudders and starts to rise, her venomous, pained words striking out at the man, who puts his hand in her face and shoves her down.

"She don't have to go with 'em, does she?" says Whitaker.

"Let 'em be, man."

"If she don't wanna go with 'em why does she have to?"

"They're the closest thing we got to TV, man. I'm watchin'. Dig it."

The three Vietnamese have turned from one another to study this exchange; they seem to know it deals with them.

"You gonna get that poor girl cut anyway, man, you get in their way," says the languid GI. "I'm tellin' you."

"What?"

"It's a family matter."

"Hey, Whitaker," says Lan.

"You really think they'd cut her? I mean, you sayin' they'd really do that? Cut her throat?"

"Why not?"

"Hey," says Lan again, "Whitaker." And in her tone of desperate supplication, Whitaker hears something clear and true. She prefers him to these other men—she prefers him and wants him to do something. He looks at her and her eyes tell him to duck the lie taking hold of him, the ploy that he's heard before and will hear again, the standard bullshit SOP that says that if he fails to stand up for her, it is for her benefit that he fails. He's saving her life by letting these little fuckers mess with her. Bullshit, he thinks. Bullshit. Who would know better than she would if there was any danger of them coming in the night to hurt her? And if she knew such a danger was real, would she ask him to intercede? And was she asking? The obvious answer shows the trick for what it is. The lie is so glaring it makes him ashamed to have nearly bought it. Ever since he let that fucking jerkoff mess with her, he has felt like half a man. He sees through the fading bullshit to the one simple thing he can give this girl. He will not let himself off the hook the way he already did once today. He will ask Lan what she wants. He will not impose himself on her, but these others won't either. If she wants to go with them, she can, though he knows she doesn't, for they are barely scratches in his awareness, thin presences, reedlike wrists and legs, and they are petty and cruel. The louder of the two has his fingers twisted in Lan's hair. She is squealing at him. Standing there, Whitaker gets a sudden whiff of pleasure and a touch of pity when he thinks of the anger and self-loathing these scrawny men must feel at the sight of a person of Whitaker's size. Their woman prefers the stranger. He understands; they must yearn to be tall and burly. "Hey," he says, stepping forward, and all three turn with questioning eyes.

"Lan," he says. "What you want?"

"Eeaaaaaaa?" she says.

The other American shifts his position, muttering, "Uh-oh."

"Don't worry, buddy boy," says Whitaker. "I'm on my own."

"Indeed."

Lan is standing, insolent and daring; she stomps her foot and says, "Shit."

Whitaker's move has put uncertainty into the situation. The Vietnamese men are tense beneath a guise of jovial ease. But neither Whitaker nor the two of them can any longer be certain of the condition in which they will leave this moment. The effect of his arrival has strengthened Lan while weakening the others. The man who clutched her wrist is hesitant about grabbing her again.

"What you want?" he says again.

She does not respond for a moment as she and the men are illuminated with a flash of headlights, while a truck and trailer-load of bombs en route to the air base roars past. The beams shred on the walls, their faces, and the earth quakes a little.

"Lan," says Whitaker.

Her fearful expression transforms to disgust and then joy as she faces him. Her grin delights him. "Numba ten," she says. "They numba fuckin' ten."

"For sure," he says.

"*Di di mau.*"

"*Di di mau,*" says Whitaker. "Get outta here," and like ghosts they go, retreating from his voice as if his voice controls them. They vanish among the shanties with a swiftness Whitaker did not anticipate, leaving the other GI chuckling in an eerily amused and lazy voice as he rises to begin his own departure.

"*Chao co,*" he says to Lan, and then he gives Whitaker a look and says, "*Chao ong.*" He's called Whitaker "Mister" in Vietnamese, delivering a half-assed dig because Whitaker has behaved decently toward a slope whore. The kid's small-minded ignorance amuses Whitaker. He will refuse the insult. He will refuse everything about it. Whitaker will drink a slow beer before traveling leisurely back to the compound in a glow of self-respect for having acted as he believes he should.

Now the dark thickens into night and the lure of Lan's body grows with the passing time. Seated on his lap, she tells him about the Vietnamese soldiers, while a stranger with a case of trinkets and a gleefully demented grin arrives from the road. "Talk me do him no money," she says. "Numba fuckin' ten do him no money. Okay. For sure. I talk him, 'No sweat, gimme tee-tee money.' 'No money,' him say. 'Shit,' I say. 'No money, bulls'it.' You know, bulls'it." The peddler sets his case open on the tabletop close by, and at the sight of his display Lan thrills and squirms, even as she is unable to quit her explanation without making sure the injustice of what happened is fully clear. "Him no can be nice. Boucoup Cheap Charlies," she says. "*Sau, sau, sau.* Must have money. No money, numba fuckin' ten. Crazy," she says. She pats her head where the one pulled her hair. "Hurt Lan." Waving her fingers over the colorful tray of cosmetics and jewelry, she peeks up at him, "You buy, okay? Okay, Whitaker?"

With the same old pouting look operating on him again, as if he's nobody, as if he just walked in, he begins to wonder just how stupid she thinks he is. As she stands and leans over the peddler, resentment heats up in him at what seems her increasingly presumptuous demands. She examines the beads, the rings and bracelets. She giggles and speaks excitedly, patting the old man's hand, and a thought comes to Whitaker as if from the back of her thin neck, the slant of her shoulders bowed over the booty she loves: she is working him like a hustler. He's a patsy for a fucking whore. In bright-eyed delight, she presents to him a blue plastic compact containing a fluffy powder puff, a silver mirror, and pink powder. "You buy me, Whitaker? Give him money."

Deciding that with this request she is sabotaging the terms between them, which began with his desire to help her, he agrees, happy to regress, if that's what she wants, happy with the amount of arousal his prick feels, looking at the darkened indentations of her dress at her crotch. He'll get a short-time. She spins in glee while the peddler happily counts Whitaker's money and Whitaker experiences a sense of diminishment. He had wanted a kind of simple decency between them and now it is gone. As Lan clicks shut the tacky little trinket, she locks the possibility away. "Shit," he says, recalling Sharon's marriage to money. "Do short-time." He brings her face around, wanting to get things moving. The startled confusion he finds is not what he expected. Whatever strange little fire is behind her eyes makes him hesitant. "Do short-time. Now," he says.

"No."

"Yes."

"No."

"I say yes."

"No. Go my home. House me long-time."

"Your house?" he says.

"For sure. An Duc To. House me."

"Short-time," he says. "I want short-time. No can do all night." He has no overnight pass and An Duc To, a village a few miles past the Long Binh compound on the highway toward Saigon, is off-limits. It's been off-limits since day one, and though he doesn't know the reason, he feels the fear of those dark miles of road where no light shines and the turnoff to the village itself is a narrow trail into a deeper darkness.

"C'mon," she says. "We go." She closes her fingers on his wrist and pulls to get him started.

He jerks away; he glares at her, annoyed that she thought she could just grab him like that. "Fuck it," he says.

"Sure. No sweat."

"You go home. You go An Duc To. I drink beer," he says. "Beer," he calls to the owner.

"You no want all night?"

He says, "Fuck it."

"Okay, okay. Fuck it. Fuck it." Haughtiness takes her over. "Fuck it," she says, and with flourishing indignation, she picks up her purse and compact. She makes a show of slipping the compact into the purse, all the while sneaking sly looks at him. He takes a big drink of beer. She's comical, her petulance so crazily overdone, and his anger could evaporate, but her brusque, arrogant march out the door leaves him sitting there. She stomps along the bottom of the steep shoulder and then up to the road. In seconds she disappears. The darkness is a wall of overwhelming black, behind which she regards her life mournfully, he knows, and hopes for him to come to her. He sits sweating, his body sluggish under the weight of a gloom he detests. Let her wounded fucking pride go to shit, he thinks and rises to glower out the window. The slanted tin rooftops hang in a row like the teeth of a saw. Suddenly visible in the distance, a fragmentary patch of water appears and disappears. At the start of the jungle, weeds stand in outline, reminding him once more of saw blades, underbrush mixing with shadows below trees and the buried moon. He can think of nothing but the trickery of women. Did he really want some genuine feeling between himself and this girl? Or was it just pity? That'd be his bet. Pity. And it's a waste on somebody like her. Maybe he could do something else decent—help out some kids, help them go to school. The rest is so shitty and complicated and messed up. When she sits down beside him, his thoughts don't stop their spinning instantly. He's no longer by the window but back at the table, and he looks up to hear her whispering softly, apology in her voice, petition in her breath on his ear and throat. "Go my house, me, Whitaker. No go short-time. Go short-time must go Madame Lieu. Go her house short-time must pay money Madame Lieu. Go house me, no money. Numba one, no money."

"Oh," he says.

"Okay?"

"Okay."

By the time they reach the road, he's not so sure. Haunted by a vague premonition of error, he watches her hail a Lambretta.

Together they climb into the back and sit on opposite sides. The headlight flares; the sputtering engine jerks them into motion. While Lan chats with the driver, Whitaker stares glumly at the rattling floor. Then, touched by a fluttering he knows to be her fingers, he looks into her shadowy face. A fleeting roadside glimmer lets him see joyful eyes. There's happiness here that he doesn't understand but wants to share. What's troubling him is the fact that it's only a few hours since he vowed to be more responsible, and not only when he got back stateside, but here, too, and already he is heading to an off-limits village when he should be getting back to the compound. But what he's doing is what he wants. Deep down he knows it. Deep down his urge is to break loose the instant he feels hemmed in, knocking aside every rule, even his own. How will he ever amount to anything?

Only the sickly yellow throw of the Lambretta's headlight lessens the inky road carrying them along between stretches of jungle, fields, a few scattered houses. With the village of Tam Hiep behind them, they pause at an intersection under four streetlights. To continue straight would carry them toward Vung Tau. They turn right, as they should, and Whitaker is reminded of the recent calamity of four air force NCOs who decided one drunken night to drive to Vung Tau for an ocean swim. The husk of their scorched, overturned jeep was found at the edge of the jungle where it had been hurled by the exploding rocket. One man lay crushed beneath it. Two others were in pieces. The fourth had scrambled into the ditch where the bullets caught and dropped him.

Out of the slatted side of the humming Lambretta, Lan waves her skinny fingers toward the Long Binh compound, coming up on their left. It's all concertina wire, bunkers, and ditches, with the long shell of the evac hospital lit up in the flats and glowing tents and Quonset huts in the distance. "You work?" she asks him.

He nods. As they near the main gate with its floodlights shining down on the closed barrier in front of sandbag barricades, the bunker, and lounging guards, he knows he should tell the driver to pull over and let him out. But he just sits there, saying nothing. He doesn't want to stop as it all floats by, and soon the wider unlit highway to Saigon down which they skitter infects him with a loneliness that moves him to close his fingers around Lan's small wrist, whether for company or because he wants her near and available for his knife should there be trouble, he doesn't know. They seem almost the same thing.

The driver calls over his shoulder, and Lan responds cheerfully, leaning close to the back of his head. The high beams of a truck are visible for a long time, approaching from the opposite direction, and then the deuce and a half whooshes past. Whitaker turns around to watch it shudder off the road, where the silhouettes of multiple tents are momentarily ghostly in the headlights.

The Lambretta slows and takes a right onto the dirt of a narrow pathway. They bounce and veer, and just beyond the wreckage of an ancient automobile, something foreign and from the thirties, Whitaker thinks, they come into An Duc To. They halt, and people of all ages watch them disembark. An old man on a stool holds an infant. A young girl eats from a bowl of bone white rice beside two young men in shorts who stare, their brown shoulders shimmering. Whitaker hears the grumble of a gasoline-powered generator.

Do they like him, or hate him, these people? he wonders. Or don't they give a shit one way or the other that he is prowling on the hand of a whore between shacks and debris down the

beaten trail of what is probably their little main street? The
first row of homes gives way to a clearing where a blacksmith's
shop pulses with showering sparks. At the next cluster of huts,
one of which is Lan's, she uses her key to let them in. He stands
a moment in the partial dark before sitting down on the edge
of a wooden bed. Lan moves a burning lantern in a slow circle
to show the dirt floor, the tin of the walls, a shabby chair and
chest. "House me numba ten," she says.

"No."

"No sweat." She joins him on the bed, unzipping his fly and
lifting his prick to the air, where under her influence, it stirs.
His brain, he realizes as if rising from a dream, aches at the
center with a blunt, punishing throb. When he reaches to lift
her skirt, she stops his fingers and confronts his questioning
look with her own guilty gaze, her dismayed apology. "Pussy
me sick, Whitaker," she says.

In the occurring silence, he squints, and she moves backward until her shoulder presses against the wall. "Got sick
pussy, Whitaker," she says and this time her meaning—she is
on her period—finds its way into his brain. He thinks of entering into blood. He thinks of entering into Vietnamese blood.
Anticipation finds an unexpected warmth, and anyway, he has
a rubber this time.

"No sweat," he says, reaching to pet the taut softness of her
thighs.

"Numba ten," she cries, "numba ten." She scurries sideways
to a position beyond his reach. He is crawling toward her over
the little bed. "Black-man," she says. "Numba ten. Talk me
do him fuck-fuck. 'No,' me talk. 'Sick pussy.' Him screaming.
Hit me. 'Pussy me sick, black-man.' Numba ten. You know.
Pussy sick. Him dinky dow. Him screaming." Now she ducks

and moves until his prick is nestled in her hands once more. He takes her head and puts her mouth down near the tip, but after a time during which she has only crouched there, dumbly pressing her lips in what seems to him bewilderment, he lets her use her fingers. In a moment arousal speeds up, and then it's racing, and he rolls sideways to get between her legs. Disappointment changes her eyes and she peers up at him in fear, but it is only the position he wants and when she understands, she smiles. Her fingers happily tap and press to coax the nerves into constriction. Okay, he thinks. He wraps his arms around her. Okay. But he wants to prolong it. He wants to prolong how it feels. He wants it to go on and on. Why can't he prolong what he's feeling? He strains above her, pumping, coming, blinking. Just this once.

A little later, wide awake and lying on his side, he stares at a filigree of spider webbing. He's stupefied with exhaustion, but nothing else seems of interest. Just the glitter of those threads. Cramped in his skull is the pain of his long day without sleep. A gecko comes from out of nowhere, chirping and scampering across the ceiling. Another hangs suspended. Dissatisfaction scrapes and squeezes him, a vice grip on his skull. His restlessness is a raw abrasion. It surprises him to find her watching him. He asks for aspirin; he taps his head, makes a suffering face; he groans, "Numba ten. Head me. Numba ten." She goes to the metal chest against the wall, but it's not aspirin that she brings back. Instead she is unscrewing the lid on a tiny jar. She takes a sniff, and gives him the chance to do the same. "Okay?" she says.

The ointment has a greenish, lardy look and a foul odor, but he doesn't know what else to do, so he says, "Okay."

"Numba one." She turns him onto his belly, and climbing

astride his back, she applies cool, greasy gobs to his temples, then his neck and shoulders and along his spine. The smell coils into his nostrils where it pokes and picks at him. He wants aspirin. Thoughts of aspirin, images of bottles, mounds of white tablets, insanely euphoric slogans taunt him with a sense of deprivation. The floor beneath the bed is dirt. His head rests partially off the bed, so he stares at the dirt. He doesn't like himself. He wishes he was someone else. He has no idea who. Who? he asks, but he's already admitted that he doesn't know; he has no idea. Anybody. Any-fucking-body. He sees his watch on his dangling wrist. It's twenty minutes to curfew, and once curfew comes and goes he will be AWOL. Lan shifts on his back. She's skinny and small, but her fingers are uncannily strong and she's digging into him, finding something, squeezing it until it retreats from her intensity, trying to find a way out of him so it can get away from her. He knows he can stay the night with little risk of getting caught. Only an attack, or a practice alert at the compound, would bring his absence to light. He doesn't want to leave. He wants to stay and be somebody else. He could become him here. Some unknown somebody else. Anybody. Any-fucking-body. "Christ, I'm going," he says. "I have to go."

As he turns to lift her off, a soft hurt of disappointment suffuses her face and gives the sound she makes a downward arc. "Eaaaaaaaaa?"

"Must go compound."

"*Sau.*"

"No. Must dee-dee."

"Numba ten."

"Me no go compound, me numba ten," he says.

"You go Bien Hoa. Do bar girl. Fuck-fuck."

"No," he says. "You dinky dow."

"For sure, I know."

"Never happen." He points at his wristwatch. "No go Bien Hoa. Too late. Must go Long Binh." He taps the glass face with the speedily moving second hand beneath it. "Must go compound. You 'stand? Dee-dee mau. Dee-dee mau."

"I go," she says.

"What?"

"Ban di dau do? You go where?"

"Compound." He points, not even certain of the correct direction. Just pointing at the wall.

"No."

"Yes."

"Okay. I go. I go. Lambretta me," she squeals. "Lambretta Lan." And a wild, mischievous glee has lighted her eyes. "For sure," she yells. "Okay. Numba one. Numba one Lambretta me!"

She's a complete fucking mystery, like the weather in some far-off part of the world changing the weather where he is. Like the planets and their shifting in a horoscope, and you read it in the newspaper and say, "What the fuck?" Her wish to accompany him is bewildering.

They're dressing together. She's hurriedly changing into white cotton pajamas, while he pulls up his underwear, his pants. He slips into his T-shirt, and then the short-sleeved button-down shirt he's been wearing. His socks are still on his feet. He's too tired to resist her. She can travel along if she wants, and he'll get rid of her at the gate. Anyway, he's not going to make it without her help.

Yammering something at him, she slips into her sandals and hurries out the door. And when he looks around and sees that he's alone, something comes over him; it's eerie and cold.

He becomes angry and spiteful, like an abandoned, vengeful ghost, looking down at her purse and the little blue compact inside. He takes it, slides it into his pocket.

Lan is knocking at the door of a neighboring hut with a Lambretta parked along the side wall, when he comes out. A man answers, and she talks excitedly, pointing at Whitaker and then off into the darkness. The man goes inside and returns in a rush to start up his machine.

They rattle along the dirt trail and then bounce onto the concrete of the highway. Whitaker looks backward, down the dark to the strange glow, solitary and fading behind them, that is An Duc To. The ride doesn't smooth out the way it should now that they're on the pavement. As they pick up a little speed the shaking actually worsens, and he figures the wheels are out of alignment or an axle is bent. They sway and shudder like a small boat on rough water. The engine has an outboard motor sound. "Hope we're not too far from shore," he says to Lan. "Can you swim?" She blinks and widens her eyes, looking puzzled. "If we run out of gas," he tells her, "we'll have to row." He doesn't feel like talking pidgin English anymore. She reaches to pat his shoulder. She says something to the driver, who turns up the throttle. They jump a few yards and then hang on to a better speed. She grins and nods reassuringly. "Okay. Numba one."

The far-off cone of light above the gate becomes visible, and then gradually distinct and brighter. Lan scoots from her side of the Lambretta to his. "You go sleep. You go sleep," she says.

"For sure," says Whitaker.

She bobs her head knowingly. She giggles and pats his hand.

"Dung lye, dung lye," he says to the driver. He can see helmeted heads moving about. He's wary of getting shot by a bored or worried guard and wants to stop with room to spare. "Dung lye." They slow and then sit idling at the far edge of the wide entranceway under the bright circle of the floodlights.

One of the guards is striding out from inside the bunker. "What's goin' on?" he yells. He stops behind a waist-high barricade, a sort of foxhole constructed of piled-up sandbags, where another guard joins him. A third guard watches through a firing slot, his rifle aimed casually in Whitaker's direction.

Whitaker climbs out quickly and waves. "Be there in a minute," he yells, busy giving money to the driver.

"Just get your butt in here, okay?" says the guard. "Snap to it." He's coming a few yards down the sloping dirt, his weapon at port arms.

"Go sleep," Lan says. Her grin is huge and real with some welling of bewildering joy Whitaker does not feel.

"Okay," he says and starts away. The Lambretta gives a high-pitched whine and then, with a grinding, suffering sound, it trundles in a circle, the jolly driver smiling and Lan nodding and waving through the slats. The broad-faced guard and his buddy are both eyeing Whitaker with a lot of interest, and so Whitaker isn't watching as Lan, gesturing toward him, disappears. He stops and looks down the highway. He can hear the struggling motor, but the Lambretta is mere white streaks becoming no more than an impression of streaks and then nothing. He thinks her slight body bounced back and forth, her arm uplifted. Is there any doubt that she rode to the gate to make sure he wasn't going to any other girl? He feels like the brunt of a joke. Hands on hips, he looks at his scuffed shoes in the gravel. The guards are counting down the seconds of the last minute before he's late, and they're at nineteen. She drew him to her house when she was on her period. He found her sitting in clean, pretty clothing, careful makeup and perfume, when she had been wearing slacks and a shirt at the time that soldier beat her. She dressed up and then sat around like she was expecting somebody. Maybe she was and they didn't show up. He springs forward the last few yards and slides sideways, his feet throwing up dust, like a baseball player coming into a base standing up. He scoots his hands outward in an umpire's signal and says, "Safe!"

The third guard has come to the door of the bunker. "You must be somethin', buddy boy," he says. He's stocky, close to the ground, almost square. "Really, really something. You got 'em followin' you home."

"I hold my breath," Whitaker says.

"You what?"

"It's the balloon principle, man. Deep breaths. All in. Not out. Never out. All that air in and in my prick so it's gettin' bigger, like a balloon. Never out. Remember the principle. Drives 'em wild."

He walks on, slowing down, like he doesn't know exactly where he is, but he's glad to be there. The rooftops of the Quonset huts are little more than glinting edges against the deep sky. The evac hospital has lots of lights on. He fingers the compact in his pocket. He should have given it back to her before she drove off. What got into him? A jeep passes, and he follows it to the motor pool. He stands looking in at the increasing number of vehicles: ambulances, jeeps, the ever-present deuce and a half, but lots of those little cargo trucks, too, some dump trucks. There are trailers and different kinds of construction equipment, a bulldozer, some backhoes. He sees a cement mixer, forklifts, a road grader. The machines stand silent and shadowy, looking almost lonely, and then the figure of a man, a sentry, strolls from behind the bulky shape of an ambulance, and here and there a hood or a fender reflects a dusty sparkle under the clouded sky, the faint starlight. They'll need him to work there soon. They have to. At least that guy walking over there has something worthwhile to guard. It won't be long. As he turns to go, he hears chords of music, a big orchestra. He looks about. What could it be? Beyond some tents he spies a bell of light. Oh, a movie's on. He glances at his watch. He'll go down. As he gets nearer, edging around some tents, he sees the film is in color. He stops for a beer in the EM club. He buys some peanuts. He plays some pinball.

22

Lan helps her neighbor, Huynh, secure his Lambretta. She thanks him and he shrugs and smiles, then goes inside. The pang that stops her short of her door is the realization that she forgot the photograph, that she left it lying in its envelope on the table with her book in Madame Lieu's sister's house. Her uncle Khiem hadn't come as he had promised and then she saw Whitaker. Well, tomorrow, she thinks, hoping the photo will be safe. They come out of the shadows as she enters, thrusting a rag in her mouth and a sack over her head when the door has been opened and closed, and she is being dragged to the ground and the bed where each takes a turn binding her arms while the other thrusts himself between her legs, stripped of her slacks and the pink cloth of her underwear, before the knife is put behind her ear and pushed so the skin opens like a seam and her gargling cry begins and ends in surprise, far off behind rags and cloth and hands. What had her? Something had her. There is pain and struggling thoughts trying to catch up, trying to answer, running wildly toward what's happening to her, but they cannot get there. The pain hammers and shatters the thoughts and they give up. What had her? Was it the wind? Did the wind have her? Did her father see her? Where would she be without the dusty world?

23

Children are scampering around on hills of glittering garbage.
Varied colors flash in the daylight, bits and pieces, irregular
shapes. It's a teetering bluff of junk spread over twenty or
thirty square yards and there are two peaks, one a bit lower
than the other. A boy in blue shorts is tossing objects down to
a pair of small girls in ragged slacks and shirts. They wait on
the level ground, looking up. He throws a box, and several tin
cans follow. They land heavily, the way they would if full. A
five-gallon gas can gets flung, then a bicycle wheel, spinning
toward the girls who scamper out of the way. On the shorter
of the two heaps, where the rubble is mostly green, two bodies
struggle over some item that Whitaker, riding shotgun on a
run to the dump, cannot identify. He and Doland, the driver,
are bouncing along toward the low-flung haze up ahead. It's

a ditch full of burning debris tended by a dozen mamasans in black pajamas and conical hats. The mamasans work along the length of the ditch with rakes and shovels. When Doland finds an open slot and prepares to back in, Whitaker jumps out. He guides Doland with hand signals and then yells for him to halt as the rear starts to overhang the drop-off. The heat comes at him like a boiling wind. He lowers the gate and swings aboard. Doland joins him, and they start dragging the first of their trash barrels to the end of the truck. They lift and empty it, and then go after the others. The fumes sting Whitaker's eyes and the exertion gets him panting. Each biting breath comes more and more rapidly into his throat. If they go slower they'll breathe easier, but be there longer. Several tires have caught fire; they send up sooty corkscrews of stink into the bright, breezeless glare.

"You know what I need?" says Doland. "A smoke."

"Fucking A," says Whitaker. "Why not?" They light up. They are part of a line of about ten trucks from various units all emptying barrels of rubbish. The deuce and a half next to them guns its engine and goes. Several others are bouncing toward them over the dry, flat terrain. A couple of mamasans scurry up. They use their rakes and shovels to push into the trench whatever rubble spilled or was dumped sloppily. Whitaker flicks his finger and sends the cigarette butt high; he loses it in the glare, then locates it, tumbling into the mess.

Later, it looks like there are even more kids working the piles of trash. Whitaker, swaying with each jolt the truck undergoes, holds his rifle with the butt balanced on the seat between his legs, the barrel out the window into the open air. He catches the stench of rot; maybe they're passing closer on their way out for some reason. One of the kids is tumbling down the steep rubble, toward the little plateau between the two piles. Whitaker, following the kid's fall, glimpses a shanty on the other side of the gap, the roof supporting a blue sign with red-painted letters spelling out something in Vietnamese. "You think that says 'garbage' in Vietnamese, Doland?"

"What?"

"That sign."

"What sign?"

"It was back there. It's gone now."

"I got to get this sucker washed before I turn it in," says Doland. "Sergeant Emlin's orders."

"Hey," says Whitaker. "Lemme tell you where."

"I know where."

"No, no. I know a really good place."

"I'm talkin' about a good enough place. I got a good place."

"You gotta listen to me, Doland."

"Why?"

"I'm tellin' you, Doland. C'mon."

"We are not gettin' laid."

"No, no. It's just a good place."

"What's good about it?"

"You know."

"If I give in to you and take you where you want, we're not gettin' laid, okay? We don't have any leeway. I got to get this vehicle turned in on time and spit-polished clean. Sergeant Emlin's got his eye on me. All of a sudden he don't like me— he's this vulture every move I make."

"No sweat. I don't have time either. I got to get back for some early chow and then I'm riding shotgun for Leahy on a run to Saigon."

"Who the hell do they think you are, Whitaker?"

"Whatta you mean?"

"You're shotgun with me and then with Leahy. Do they think you're some kinda gunslinger?"

"They just don't know what to do with me. That's my guess."

Other car washes start showing up long before Madame Lieu's. Doland eyes each new opportunity as it whizzes by, like he knows he should veer into the next one he sees. Whitaker keeps saying, "It's just a little farther."

The midmorning sun is fierce, the sky a flat, empty blast of blue. Lots of military vehicles are cranking along in both directions, and so are Vietnamese on bicycles, motor scooters, and on foot. Whitaker doesn't know exactly what he's doing. He doesn't have the compact on him. He's not even sure he wants to give it back, because that would let her know he took it. He's just curious, is how it feels to him.

"Can I ask you somethin', Whitaker? And you can't laugh."

"Why not? What if it's funny?"

"The doc says I got to get circumcised. Do you think I should? What would you do if you were me?"

"How come you're not circumcised, Doland?"

"What do you mean? How do I know? They didn't do it. But the doc says that's why I keep getting the clap, and if I get circumcised I won't get it as often."

"That's a rock and a hard place, man."

"I hate gettin' those shots in the ass. But gettin' circumcised has gotta hurt, too."

"Are you gonna do it?"

Making a dangerously wide exit out of somewhere, another deuce and a half is broadside in front of them, and Doland honks and steers almost onto the shoulder and then back to safety. The shiny truck, water dripping off the running boards, shoots past. The car wash it just departed flies by on the right. "What's wrong with that place?"

"It's just a little farther."

"You keep saying that. Why am I doin' this?" Doland asks, sounding sad.

"It's just around that corner up there." He's claiming more certainty than he has, but the dust billowing up and swirling away, the bedraggled palm trees bunched close to the road look like things he's seen before, and he probably has. But they could have been anywhere along this miserable road. He undergoes a funny excitement as the gentle bend clears the drooping fronds and the little blue building comes into view. A soap-splashed jeep sits on the dark, damp gravel, kids with buckets and rags are running around. "That's it," he says. "We're here."

There's room beside the jeep, and almost before the engine shuts off, kids emerge from behind the building where they were probably gambling or goofing off. They smile at Doland and Whitaker and jabber at one another, scampering around to get their buckets. "Keep your eye on my weapon. I'll get us some Cokes," says Whitaker.

He's hoping that Lan will simply appear, that he will turn and see her the way he did when she was inside that window watching him. He goes up to the blue building and peeks in the window. There's a chunky girl with pretty big tits on the lap of a GI, and he can hear another girl, who doesn't sound like Lan, tittering. He steps in and the GI smiles at him. The tittering girl is nestled across the thighs of a big roly-poly soldier. She has her back to Whitaker, but he can tell she's giving the guy a hand job. A third girl looks up from her magazine. "Hey, GI," she says, and the roly-poly guy peeks around his whore; he's flushed and looks confused.

"Gimme two Cokes," Whitaker says to the girl whose wide face and bright black eyes have a kind of dazzle that she lets him see, then takes away, aiming her butt cheeks at him as she bends to the washtub full of melting ice chips and Cokes.

The roly-poly guy sputters and kind of bounces on the wicker chair. *"Troi oi,"* says the girl; the chair wobbles and creaks; she wraps both arms around his big head and gives him a squeeze. His buddy is laughing and standing up. "You had enough, Pollard?" he says. He has a clean-cut look to him, Whitaker realizes, neat blond hair, clear blue eyes, tailored fatigues, like he thinks he's an officer.

"Oh, man, Blake, I'm feelin' kinda faint," says Pollard. "What is wrong with these girls?"

Off him now, the girl is giving her palm a wincing, disgusted look. "Numba ten," she says, then swirls her hand in the washtub so the ice chips and bottles rattle around.

Pollard grabs a magazine to shield the dark stain near his fly as they go. "That was crazy, man. Blake, did you see what she did?"

"She gave you a hand job."

The bright-eyed girl has moved close to Whitaker, holding out the bottles. "Name me Ai," she says. "You want short-time?"

He shakes his head. "Maybe later." As he pays her for the Cokes, he looks around. "Lan? Where?"

The girl smiles and shrugs. "Five hundred Ps."

"Lan," he says. "You know Lan?"

"Lan *di di,*" says the chunky one, withdrawing her hand from the water with a dripping Coke of her own.

"Di di?" he says.

"For sure." She dries her hand on the leg of her slacks.

"An dee dow?" Whitaker says. "Lan go where?"

"Toi khong biet." She makes a hapless gesture, takes a quick drink.

"Lan work Madame Lieu?" he asks. "Maybe tonight, maybe tomorrow?"

"Maybe," says the girl close to Whitaker. "For sure."

The chunky one gives an annoyed grunt and starts babbling. It's clear she's scolding the girl next to Whitaker, who shrugs and talks back. Whitaker sees how her strangely exaggerated features give her a kind of drastic beauty. But as the two of them keep squabbling, he wonders if they even know Lan. He's never seen them before. The third girl, looking fed up, goes out the door.

The truck is almost finished. He can see kids with rags on the roof and fenders. Doland stalks into view carrying the M14. Whitaker takes the arm of the girl at his side. She turns her eyes on him and they're so unusual he almost looks away. "You talk Lan. Me Whitaker." With his finger, he underscores his nametag. "Whit-a-ker. Okay? You talk Lan—Whitaker come back. Today." He's thinking that, if he's lucky, he can bring the jeep in for a quick wash after the Saigon run. "You talk Lan, Whitaker come back."

"Okay," she says.

The deuce and a half honks loudly. Doland is on the running board, leaning in the open door to punch the horn.

"Okay?" he says to the girl. "Same-same today."

The other one brightens and chimes in, "Okay. For sure."

The instant Whitaker steps into the yard, Doland piles into the cab, and Whitaker catches sight of Madame Lieu walking with the third whore along the path that leads back from the shanties. "Mamasan, mamasan." He hurries to her, towers over her, "Lan," he says. "Lan work tonight?" The rumbling deuce and a half is ready to go. Madame Lieu is scrawny and a little crooked the way she stands, her hair pulled so tight over the top of her head it's like a rubber mat. She wears black pajama bottoms and a faded purple shirt that droops down her flat chest and flatter belly. Her face is furrowed, with wrinkles like claw marks. She stares at him. Whitaker points to his nametag. "Name me Whitaker."

"Okay. For sure. You want short-time Ai? She boucoup *dep. Dep, dep.*"

"Maybe later."

Doland honks three more times.

Mamasan pats the forearm of the whore at her side. "You short-time Ngu?"

"I talk you Lan. You talk Lan. Me come back. See Lan. Same-same today."

"*Toi khong biet.*"

"For sure."

"Ai numba one short-time girl. You do fuck-fuck Ai."

Doland has enlisted some kid to help him back out safely onto the road. Whitaker turns and runs. He bounds up and into the truck as it starts forward. "You weren't really going to leave without me, were you?"

Doland is shifting into second gear. "Don't talk to me, you idiot. I don't want to talk to you. You make me feel like a jerk."

"Whatta you mean?"

"Just shut up! I mean it! Not another fucking word!"

So they drive in silence the whole way back to the base. Doland lets him out and Whitaker barely hits the ground before Doland says, "Shut the damn door."

He slams it.

"And you forgot the Cokes, too. You didn't even bring me my fucking Coke, man."

What an asshole, Whitaker thinks, standing at the side of the company street watching the truck drive off. He shakes his head. "What the hell." But he doesn't have any time to waste worrying about Doland. There's a lot he needs to get done. He has to turn in his two magazines of rounds to Sergeant Cross, then get over to the mess hall for early lunch. He has to find time for a shower, too, because he reeks of burning trash. He's supposed to meet Leahy, ready to go at eleven so they can pick up the officer they're chauffeuring to Saigon. And he has to be sure to remember to get back to Cross and pick up the two magazines when it's time to go.

The cooks have been notified to feed him early, so he has no trouble there. He downs two cheeseburgers with tons of catsup and piles of fried potatoes, piles of pickles, some orange juice, and several cups of coffee. The shower is rushed, but he's thankful to put on clean fatigues. He sticks the compact into his pocket and remembers to stop back for his ammunition. He's cutting it close, but on time, even a few minutes early when he arrives where Leahy told him to wait, just above the evac hospital's officers' billets. Leahy isn't there. But that's okay. Whitaker's early. He checks his watch. A few minutes go by. He starts to worry that he's in the wrong place, even though he knows he isn't. Another few minutes go by. Still, no Leahy. He looks down the road in one direction and then the other. The guy's a boozer. Everybody knows it.

He hears a faint motor sound overhead. A chopper is coming in from the north. It speeds toward him, the thump-thump of the blades increasing. The red cross on the side means it's a Dustoff. Whitaker is on slightly higher ground, so he's look-

ing down at the landing pad. The medevac is looping south
and reversing. That morning when he and Doland were collecting barrels to take to the dump, they saw a formation of
helicopters going north in the otherwise empty blue sky. They
stopped what they were doing and stood, heads tilted back,
hands shielding their eyes. One or two at first and then more
and more came on, the noise building, until a long column of
choppers filled the sky floating side by side, with others above
and below, each loaded with troopers, like a squadron of
greenish insects advancing slowly. It went on like that, while
Whitaker and Doland traveled around to different sites picking up trash. They were straining to lift a particularly cumbersome barrel, when Whitaker glanced up just as the last of the
choppers, looking forsaken by the others, struggled from view,
and the empty sky was silent again. Word spread that it was
the 173rd Airborne headed out on an operation. This Dustoff
must be casualties coming in. It plummets in a small storm of
wind and debris, then halts, swaying above the gigantic red
cross painted on concrete so sun blasted it looks white. Down
comes the dark, slow shadow. A flurry of smaller shadows
skate and scurry. The skids touch, lift, and settle.

Hatless litter bearers scramble from under the awning at
the entrance to the hospital. Ducking low, dark sweat blotch-
ing their backs, they plow into the wind thrown up from the
churning rotors. One of the bearers, a Pfc, motions in the direction of the awning. A stocky Spec Four hurries out. There's
no sound other than the motor, the whistle of the blades. The
Pfc and Spec Four come out from behind the medevac with
a stretcher bearing a blue-green body bag. KIA. Some poor
dead fuck. The next casualty looks dead, too; he's that limp,
just this green blob of tattered fatigues with a little pink face,

his chest wrapped in stained bandages, and a medic carrying the IV hooked to his arm. They're hurrying and he bounces. The helicopter roars; the tail rises, settles. Transporting a second body bag is causing problems; they don't have a stretcher; the weight keeps shifting, almost pulling the bag out of their grasp. It drags along the pavement, until the Pfc runs back out and grabs it under the middle. The chopper bounces, then leans and lifts through a hundred and then two hundred gleaming feet of sky, and leveling there, it turns to run, nose at a slight downward pitch, back to the north.

It's another fifteen minutes before Leahy pulls up. He tells Whitaker to get in and that the officer was delayed by some bullshit. "This doctor is a shrink," Leahy says and rolls his eyes. They're supposed to pick him up over by the mess hall where he went to grab something quick. "From what I hear, some colonel at MACV has gone off the deep end, so this captain is going in to babysit him. Can you believe it? I can't."

"No," Whitaker says. He tries to get a whiff of the air between them just in case there's alcohol on Leahy's breath, but all he smells is spearmint from the gum Leahy's chomping. He's hawk faced, with long black eyebrows, a thirty-five-year-old Pfc who saw the worst of it in Korea as a rifleman when the Chinese infantry poured across the border. Everybody knows his story, because he tells them, how he was half frozen, dead guys all over the bloody snow. He stayed in and made it to staff sergeant, but some kind of friction with a captain got out of hand and he was busted to private. And, oh yeah, he likes to drink.

"That's him," Leahy says. Their passenger is round shouldered and heavyset, with pale skin and big ears. He's standing beside a briefcase reading some documents, probably the 201 file for the MACV nut job; he has a cup of coffee and is still chewing his food when he looks over the rims of his glasses at Whitaker, who is standing beside the jeep. "Hello, son."

"Yes, sir. Hello, sir."

"Let's take Highway One," he says to Leahy.

"Yes, sir."

"Do know how to get to MACV that way?"

"Yes, sir."

"Is there another way you'd prefer?"

"No, sir."

As they cruise out the gate, Whitaker figures he better stay sharp, so he plants the butt of the rifle on the seat, angles the barrel to the sky, and sits up straight. The captain doesn't say another word, and his presence seems to make Leahy tight-lipped and uneasy. They go a while, nobody making a sound, and then Whitaker, curious about what's going on behind him, pretends to stretch. The captain has stopped reading and sits with his hands folded on his belly, like he's praying or maybe sleeping behind the big sunglasses he's put on.

The traffic gets crazy. It's honking, pedaling, careening mayhem. Whitaker thinks they must be in Saigon. He's seen loony traffic before, but never anything like this. Leahy stays calm, handling the chaos with a steady, straight-ahead stare until he slides to the curb in front of MACV headquarters. The captain says nothing, climbing out and busily fussing with the sweat-stained, sticky seat of his pants. They're free to go, so they head out. Within a block, Leahy starts ranting about having to deal with primitive drivers and arrogant officers. He says something about a shortcut, then starts cursing, honking, tailgating, and cutting in between scooters, and then he pulls to the curb. "Fuck this," he says and jumps out.

"Leahy, what are you doin'?"

"I gotta take a piss. Just sit tight." He walks straight in to a bar.

Stuck at the edge of stampeding traffic honking and screeching in what seems like a dozen directions, and surrounded by street signs he can't read, Whitaker has no idea what to do other than just sit there and drip sweat. But then a Vietnamese cop car crawls by and the two white mice in their white uniforms eye him and then appear to discuss him. He clambers over to the driver's side. That way he'll look like he's waiting for somebody. And he can take off if he needs to. But take off where? Fucking Leahy. Is he supposed to track him down? He can hardly walk away and leave the jeep sitting there. And he's got his M14; he sure as hell can't leave it, and the idea of carrying it into the bar doesn't seem too bright.

The sidewalk is almost as hectic as the street, kids and old ladies, papasans pushing carts, ARVNs in uniform, gooks in business suits, and a bunch of young girls in white outfits, slacks under dresses that go down to their ankles but have slits up the side, and Leahy plowing through their ranks. Veering and reeling straight at Whitaker. He piles in, carrying two big bottles of Coke. "Let's go. You think you wanna drive, then drive." He's flushed, his eyes red rimmed and bleary; the guy is totally trashed after being gone a few minutes. "I said, 'Let's go,' Whitaker. So go. Did you hear me?"

"You gotta give me directions."

"Go straight. Here," he says, handing over one of the Cokes. "I'll drive if you want."

"No." The bottle is cool to the touch, and the first swig a godsend. He checks behind them, but there's no such thing as a break in the onslaught, so he waves his hand as if to force space between a battered truck and the scooters passing it as he takes the plunge. Everything squeals and honks and adapts to accept him.

"Get into that circle coming up, stay on the right, and when you get to the far side, bear right."

"What's the far side? It's a fucking circle!"

"I'll tell you." He puts the bottle to his lips, and Whitaker notices that Leahy's Coke is reddish rather than dark. Not merely diluted it must be mostly bourbon.

"What you got there?"

"Just drive." Leahy leans back, closing his eyes and cradling the M14 so it rests across his chest and shoulder. "That fucking captain couldn't say a word to us, could he? Not a fucking word. Whatta prick."

"He was busy. You know."

"He's a prick. He didn't talk because he knew we'd see through him. Why's he a fucking captain anyway?"

"You gotta tell me where to go."

"Fuck that."

"What?"

"Don't worry. I'm with you." He sits up, grows focused, leans forward. "You see that big red sign up ahead with the blue letters? Take a right at the corner."

They go like that, Leahy drinking and offering embittered, grumbling directions, while Whitaker obeys step after step, hoping for the best, and then Leahy looks at him and says, "You're a good boy, Whitaker. You're my boy. You're my horse, if you never win a race. Do you know where we are?"

"Not for sure."

Leahy guzzles, then purrs and closes his eyes. "This is it, trooper. Highway 1. The road home. You just stay on it and we'll be there sooner than jack shit."

Ahead of them, the traffic is advancing steadily into the dazzle of the day. "No kidding. Okay," Whitaker says. So they should be back by 1430 hours at the latest. Maybe even 1400. Something in the moment inclines Whitaker to think in army time. 1400 hours. 1430. Leahy's messed-up history, the bodies in the bloody snow, the teenaged Leahy fending off Chinese hordes, even his drinking and useless misery, makes his praise satisfying. Looking half asleep Leahy takes a tiny sip; he raises and lowers his chin in acceptance of some inner, inescapable burden, and then he rests his cheek against the hand guard of Whitaker's rifle. His damp face is glazed in sweat. Whitaker can feel his own body coming to a boil; droplets trickle down his brow, his cheeks; they fall from the tip of his nose. It's an afternoon like an explosion sending shock waves all the way to the clouds on the tattered horizon.

"I can't take it," Leahy says. "I just can't take it." He sounds hurt. "That armada this morning—it was a fucking armada."

"What?"

"I can't take it. Did you see 'em?"

"Whatta you mean?"

"The choppers—the 173rd on its way out into—"

"Oh. You mean the choppers, all the—"

"I mean that fucking armada, it was a fucking armada. Wake the fuck up!"

"Yeah, yeah. It was unbelievable."

"It's all kids, all kinds of poor kids out there—kids tryin' to learn what I already know, tryin' to learn it and gettin' killed tryin'. It ain't right. I should be there. I should be with 'em, teachin' 'em. I could keep maybe just one of 'em alive and he could go home, you know, he could go home and have a date and get laid by some nice round-eyed girl. It should be me in a body bag comin' back—it should be me in 'em. At least one of 'em. It should be me, and then that one, that kid could go home."

He wraps his arms around the rifle, hugging it, squeezing; the barrel indents his cheek. He strains violently. "Fuck," he says. "Fuck, fuck . . ." He drops the rifle, and wheels around and stands up. Whitaker fears Leahy is going to jump, and then, realizing he is headed for the backseat, Whitaker awaits an accidental drunken tumble to the road. But Leahy lands where he aimed.

Whitaker is holding the rifle, which he grabbed without even thinking while tracking Leahy and steering.

"You think I'm drunk out of my mind, don't you, Whitaker," says Leahy. "Don't you. Admit it."

"Yes I do," he says.

"Well, you are right. Give yourself a fucking prize."

He cranes his neck to find Leahy curling up on his side. "I'm goin' to sleep."

The traffic is moving even more swiftly than before. Whitaker sees Vietnamese in trucks, which look like they're coming apart even as they bounce along, water buffalo trudging the shoulder with some farmer waving a stick, even couples and families dressed up and walking into a kind of picnic area. When he spots U.S. Army vehicles, he takes them as a good sign. But he still wakes Leahy a couple of times to confirm where they are. Leahy sits up, blinking, sweating, and scanning the countryside, before saying, as if the answer is obvious, "Yeah, yeah." Then he flops back down. Whitaker is glad it's daylight and hopeful Leahy knows what he's talking about, but it's still a kind of shock when the gate to the compound shows up on the right. He tells Leahy to wake up; he better sit up straight.

Once they pull to a halt in their area, he ditches the empty Coke bottles and brings a tray balancing as many coffees as he can carry to Leahy, who sits on the side of his bunk with his head bowed drinking the first one. He smiles at Whitaker; he winks; his dazed, lopsided expression struggles to offer several versions of wordless approval.

"I'll go get the jeep washed and then come back and meet you here, okay, and we'll go turn it in."

"You're my boy, Whitaker. You're my horse," Leahy says. "We're not dead. We're not dead."

It's funny, but without thinking about Lan he has become eager to see her. He knows she'll be there; he has the same lucky feeling he had the first time he ran into her. He tries to remember, tries to see it again, the road, the dark, that faint headlight on her.

The gravel area at Madame Lieu's is packed with a deuce and a half and a jeep getting soaked and scrubbed, while another jeep waits, so he parks a little farther on. It's a dry bumpy pocket of dust in front of somebody's house. He left his rifle at the compound; he turned in the ammo, so he's free of those worries. He tosses and catches the key before tucking it away. He feels almost nervous. The yard teems with kids piling on and off the vehicles, scurrying around, shrill and shirtless. A GI sits smoking in the jeep that's waiting. There's a lot of noise coming from the bar. A whore in red pedal pushers steps out, and though her build is similar to that of Lan, he knows it's not her. They all have black hair. A rawboned corporal is right behind her, pushing her along. Mysteriously, the corporal glares at Whitaker. They've never met. The guy staggers, sends a bullshit salute in Whitaker's direction. He corrals the whore's waist with both hands and makes her go faster.

At least two radios are blasting inside the blue building, one of them with that bouncy *Up on the Roof*. The other is this bunch of black guys wailing away about reaching out, they'll be there. He knows to prepare, to get ready in case he finds her busy, maybe on somebody's lap. It's not to give her the compact that he's there, he realizes. Or is it? Why is he there? And he laughs. To get laid, like everybody else.

Maybe six GIs—a mix of blacks and whites—and four whores crowd the sweltering space, their rambunctious, fidgety bodies making a forbidding impression, as if they are triple that number. First he recognizes the whore with the strange eyes, and then he sees the chunky one. The other two he doesn't know. It seems that nobody is tending the washtub of beer, so he plucks out a bottle.

"Don't steal from these little fuckers!" one of the GIs sneers. "Because we are guests in their fucked-up country."

Whitaker smiles and shows the money. Ai sees him and calls, "Okay, numba one. You give one hundred twenty, okay?"

"We got to respect their customs and traditions no matter how sick and fucking perverted they are!" the GI says. He looks about fifteen, peach fuzz and disbelief at how angry he is; he has his hand on the chunky whore's shoulder, her collarbone. Like everyone in the room except Whitaker, he wears a 1st Division Infantry patch above his Pfc stripe. This whole bunch is probably just back from the boonies. Maybe a squad with their corporal out back. Whitaker takes a long pull of beer, and the kid tells him, "You want to get laid, you got to wait your fucking turn. Ain't that right, Carter."

From behind the whore who straddles him, the guy who must be Carter says, "What?"

The kid isn't really paying attention. He's fixed on his

whore, putting one hand on either side of her head and staring drunkenly into her eyes. He lifts her hair on both sides until it extends outward like wings that he lets fall.

Whitaker slips outside. He'll come back some other time. Lan isn't there, or if she is, she's working in one of the shanties. He really has no idea why he's there anyway. Did he have something in mind? If he did, he no longer knows what it was. He can stop and get the jeep cleaned at some other place along the way. He's seated behind the wheel ready to turn the key when Madame Lieu steps out of a door just below where he parked. She sees him and stops; she stares strangely before retreating inside. Her look, the flash of her eyes as they found him, has left something maddening behind. He has no idea what it is, and even less of an idea what is prompting his irritation, but he can feel his temper rising. He's marching down to talk to her when he realizes that the orange house he's approaching is the one in which he saw Lan sitting in the window. It's right there in front of him with its wooden shutters wide open. He can hear Madame Lieu jabbering behind the wall. He steps up, his fingers on the orange stone of the sill, as he peers in. She's only a few feet away talking to someone he can't see. "Hello," he says.

She squints at him. "Lan say talk you short-time Ai. Lan say Ai numba one. Lan numba one. Ai numba one."

His impulse to respond is confused by doubt that he heard right. "Mamasan. Lan an di dow, okay?"

Looking annoyed, she starts jabbering, heatedly, but it's not to him. Dressed in black slacks and a neatly white buttoned dress shirt, a young man steps forward and stands beside her. "Hello," he says.

"Hello."

"Lan gone to Vung Tau," he says. "You know Vung Tau? Vung Tau ocean. Water."

Whitaker nods. "Okay."

"Very nice. Good. She go Vung Tau. Not coming back. Go live Vung Tau. Very nice. You know. Sand. Ocean, water."

"Oh," says Whitaker. "Oh."

"Yes. Very nice."

The old woman drifts deeper into the room. At a doorway with curtains, which she holds partly open, she chatters for a few seconds. A small boy in shorts and bare feet comes out, crossing the brown, square tiles of the floor. He emerges from the door, and runs, following a path that climbs behind neighboring homes in the direction of the bar. Madame Lieu is talking intently to the young man; she seems to be offering a small white envelope for him to take.

"Okay, okay," he says to her.

She scuttles in her crooked way to a position just inside the window, where she delivers a singsong speech aimed right at Whitaker. Finished, she looks hopefully to the young man, who eases up and shows Whitaker the envelope he took from her. "You see?" he says. "Lan say give you. Lan say you—she say Whitaker." He scribbles his finger under his own breast pocket, then aims the finger at Whitaker's nametag. "She say, 'Whitaker come Vung Tau. See her sometime. Okay? You understand?"

"Okay."

"She say give you." He slides out a black-and-white photograph of a girl in a long tunic that falls to her ankles. "She say you numba one. Give you." It's Lan in the picture, and she is all dressed up. It takes him a second to realize that her clothing is similar to what he saw those young girls wearing in Saigon earlier, those slim white outer garments slit up the side to reveal white slacks. Though he can't identify the actual color of Lan's dress because the black-and-white photo makes it merely dark, he knows it's not white. "You see?" says the young man, and he carefully touches the image of the dress with his finger. "*Ao Dai.* Numba one. Very pretty. Okay? She say give Whitaker." He eases the photograph back where it came from, and busies himself fixing the clasp. "She say you look, you see her. You can think her Vung Tau."

So it all comes clear; Lan has moved to Vung Tau. As he accepts the envelope, he tries to remember the words for thank you, but all that comes to mind is *"Xin Loi,"* which is "sorry."

Savage, hair-raising shouts startle them. The deuce and a half is loading up the last of the First Infantry squad. One of them stands shirtless, drumming on the roof of the cab. As the truck pulls out, they sprawl on the benches along the sides; they lean over the rails, hooting like wild men. Some of them see Whitaker looking, and one of them gives him the finger. Quickly, the truck gathers speed, and in the plume of dust it leaves behind, their cries fade. The kid Madame Lieu sent off is coming down the path, leading Ai by the hand.

"Ai numba one," says Madame Lieu. "Lan say you short-time Ai."

The young man smiles. "Nice we talk you, okay?"

"Okay."

His dark eyes brighten. "Lan say you short-time Ai. You no be sad." He smiles in a different way, adding a nod before departing for the other room.

As Ai gets closer, she looks past Whitaker to Madame Lieu. The old woman is coming out the door, gesturing impatiently. The kid scampers up and she bends to him with a high-pitched jab of a sentence, then shoves him toward the road. Whitaker's jeep is being surrounded by a crew of kids with buckets and rags. The kid sprints to join them.

Watching the GI walk off with Ai, Madame Lieu thinks how much trouble this has been. Doing what's right has been very difficult for her. But he will go home soon. The sadness of life will find him there, or here. Who knows? Only Heaven can say. She feels lucky, though, even blessed by the good fortune that brought her son for a visit, when his English was so necessary, so useful. By helping his mother, by making her task possible, Du's presence seems to confirm the rightness of her actions. She did as she was taught when a child, as she fervently believes people should do, as she taught her children. Manners require that a decent person conceal news of misfortune whenever possible. Since nothing could be done to change how Lan died, what benefit was there in speaking of it? In their hearts, people want to be reassured, to have their minds put at ease, even if what is kept from them is very bad. Other GIs had asked for Lan, but this one asked and came back. It was too many times. The others asked, but when Lan could not be found, they forgot about her. Now he will forget, too. Everyone will suffer in time, as Heaven sees fit. Should Lan's uncle appear, she will protect him in the same way, explaining that his niece brought the photograph just as he requested, but it was stolen by a drunken GI.

In the shanty where Ai takes Whitaker, she holds out her hand for the money, and then makes it clear she doesn't want to remove her blouse. Her hair is thick, black, almost shoulder length; the ends curl inward to her neck and have a final tiny upward swoop on each side; her bangs, almost long enough to cover her eyes, part unevenly the first time she brushes them aside, and then exactly in the middle the next time. It takes a while for him to get going, but it happens eventually. Looking up, she has those high cheekbones and drastic eyes. This is what he came for, he thinks, and after a while it is.

When he walks to his jeep, the sky has darkened, and the kids are working on a truck in front of the bar. A jeep sits waiting. One of the whores runs up to the guy behind the wheel. She hands him a Coke, then leans in close. She giggles and scurries away, and Whitaker feels that he's at a Dairy Queen with girls running around bringing burgers and fries, and the whores are carhops. Back at the compound, he finds Leahy sacked out, violently snoring. Whitaker shakes him for a while before Leahy finally sits up, looking desperate, almost panicky. His eyes are bloodshot, his skin pale. Whitaker explains that Leahy signed the jeep out, so he has to sign it back in. Leahy struggles to pull on his trousers and loses his balance. He sits down on his bed, then rushes outside and bends over a trash barrel, but he doesn't puke. Whitaker notices that dark clouds are visible now, gathering, thickening. By the time they're done with the jeep, the sky is black. Beyond layers of mist odd figures are taking shape. Leahy looks lost; he has stopped walking. They're in the middle of the road. Whitaker stands beside him. Leahy puts his hands on his hips. He says he feels half dead; he says that a Mongol horde is marching through his mouth with only their dirty socks on. He weaves and wobbles as they cross over a corrugated metal strip bridging a drainage ditch. When he gets to the other side, he says that he thinks he needs to eat something. He wants Whitaker to go with him. Just before they enter the mess hall, Whitaker's backward glance shows a sky in disarray, gigantic inky splotches, towering funnel-like spirals, beams of falling light being beaten back, swept aside. Leahy thinks he ought to start slow, maybe just some bread and tomato juice. He asks one of the cooks with whom he goes back a long ways to toast the bread for him. Whitaker loads his tray with beef stew, string beans, some cooked carrots, French fries. Leahy thinks the stew smells okay to him, so maybe he'll try it. He gets to his feet and smiles, as if standing is a huge accomplishment. Past him Whitaker sees Sergeant Emlin a few steps inside the door. Emlin scans the mess hall, his eyes roving from table to table in a determined manner that makes Whitaker know to duck and hope to go unnoticed. He remains stock-still, eyes averted, until he hears signs of someone approaching. Sergeant Emlin stands over him. "Whitaker. We need a replacement on gate guard. Collins is puking his guts out. He hadda go on sick call."

"Aww, Sarge. C'mon."

"C'mon what? Let's go. Eat up and get a move on."

"I had a long, hard day."

"Listen to this asshole," he says to Leahy, who has come back with a little stew on his tray. "Tell him, Leahy. He thinks he had a hard day." He offers a disgusted momentary silence, a righteous stare. "A hard time is those troopers from the 173rd getting dropped into a fucking kill zone. A hard time is the ones coming back on stretchers or in body bags—the ones headed to the evac or the morgue. They're the ones got it hard."

"Ain't that the damn truth, Sarge," says Leahy.

Emlin eyes Leahy's tray. "What, are you on a fucking diet, Leahy?"

"Little upset stomach, Sarge."

"Cut the crap, Whitaker," Emlin says. "Report to me in twenty. You're my volunteer."

He watches Emlin all the way out the door. "Shit," he says. He glances to Leahy, who seems suddenly to dislike him.

The rain starts as he gathers up his gear. He doesn't have much time, and so none to spare, but he deserves a fucking minute, he thinks. He digs the little white envelope out of his footlocker. He sits on his bunk and looks at the photo. It's neat how sexy she is in that fancy dress. Something about the slits up the side and the high collar. He doesn't really understand it. But she seems taller, too, looking off with this kind of flirtatious expression, serious though, prim and proper, holding that flower in her hands. There are all those other flowers in vases around her. But it's the high collar that gets him, and her hands folded around the stem, like she's a prude or a bride. Except for the sexy slits up the side. That's when he knows what he'll do. It makes him laugh. He'll send it to Roger. He'll write a note telling his brother how often he gets laid and how this one is nuts about him. How he sees her all the time. How she fucks him crazy, how she does whatever he wants. He hurries to get it ready, addressing the envelope, affixing the stamp. He works carefully, writing out the note. He can just see his brother opening the envelope and being stopped in his tracks by Lan, thinking, What a hot bitch! At the last second he decides to print WAR IS HELL! across the photo, and adds his signature.

It's pouring as Whitaker leaves the mailroom and trudges down the road toward the gate, which he can barely see. The sky is a wall of gray blotting out the sun, the stars, the moon, whatever might be up there. Rain pounds on his poncho, rattling loudly; it clatters on his helmet. He carries his rifle slung so the muzzle points to the ground. His canteen and ammo pouch bounce off his hips as he shuffles along, thinking, Hut two three four. Hut two three four.

A truck, pelted and sopping, sits at the gate on its way into the compound. One of the guards stands with his head tipped steeply back so he can talk to the driver. Whitaker strides to the passenger side. The window is open and the man seated a few inches back from the frame is mostly in the shadows, but Whitaker thinks he knows him. "Hey," he says, "we were in basic together. Fort Leonard Wood, right?" The guy leans forward and he is gaunt and stricken, with strange big eyes. He seems to be going blind for the few seconds he stares at Whitaker.

The truck splashes off, uncovering the other guard. "I'm here for Collins," Whitaker tells him.

"Okay."

"I thought I knew that one."

"Did you?"

"I guess not. What'd they want?"

"They're going to visit their buddy. They're from a transportation company and their convoy got hit and he got his legs blown off."

They go into the bunker and stand staring out. Two other guards are flopped on cots in the back. One sits up and says, "I can't fucking sleep."

"It's early."

"Hey, new guy. If you sleep, keep your boots on because there's rats back in that corner."

"I think it was the same one twice."

"I think it was two different ones. Two different rats."

"You didn't take notice of any distinguishing markings, did you?"

"No."

"So maybe it was just one."

"Maybe."

"And we saw him twice. That could be."

"Sure. I guess."

Whitaker starts thinking about Lan and maybe getting a pass to go to Vung Tau. He leans on the sandbags, peering through a firing slot into the flood and fog. There are units stationed at Vung Tau, but guys go there for a kind of mini R & R sometimes. It's on the beach. After a while one of the guards heads down to the evac hospital's mess hall. He brings back egg salad sandwiches for everybody and a big thermos of coffee. Whitaker fills his canteen cup with hot black coffee. He pulls the hood of his poncho up over his head and he puts his helmet on top of the hood. He walks out of the bunker. The front and back of the poncho fall around him like the sides of a tent shuddering, but keeping him safe, under the pelting rain. He sips his coffee and feels he's missing out. He feels it deeply, powerfully, unexpectedly, senselessly. He's missing out on something, though he has no idea what it is. He's just missing out. He peers into the deluge and sips his coffee and then he feels something else. The torrent is steady. It falls in sheets, all but erasing the road. It streams off his helmet, past his eyes. Alone in his poncho, sheltered in his poncho, with coffee in the still-hot canteen cup in his hands, he has the strangest sensation that at this very moment he stands at the high point of his life. The pounding splatter on the road, on the rubber of his poncho, on his helmet sounds more like crashing waves than countless drops of water, no matter how many he tries to imagine. It's like it's falling inside his head. Pop pop. Lollipop, lollipop, oh lolli, lolli, lolli. Now he is getting mad. At what? At motherfucking what? Tonight you're mine, completely. . . . More fucking song lyrics. But by the morning, by the sun . . . when the night . . .

"Hey," one of the guards yells to him. "What are you doing out there?"

"C'mon in before you drown."

"What?"

"C'mon in before you drown."

"Don't you know enough to come in out of the rain?"

"It doesn't look like it, does it?" Whitaker yells.

"No."

"We saved you a sandwich."

"Okay. I'm comin'."

"Hurry up."

"Okay."

"Come on."

"Okay."

Acknowledgments

"Can one appeal to Heaven, so far away?" That is how the Vietnamese characters on the cover translate. They are line 596 from *Truyện Kiều, The Story of Kieu,* the great classical poem of Vietnam written in ideographic Nôm, the ancient script of Vietnam, by Nguyễn Du (1765–1820). I owe their presence and authenticity to John Balaban and Lê Văn Cường of The Vietnamese Nôm Preservation Foundation, http://nomfoundation.org. My thanks to Dick Hughes for putting me in touch with John.

At one point in the text I have paraphrased and then quoted from *Kim Van Kieu,* the prose translation of *The Story of Kieu,* rendered by Le Xuan Thuy.

Thanks to the early readers of this manuscript: Deborah Schneider and Sarah Hochman, Marsha Rabe, George Nicklesburg, Jill Rabe, Ricky Trabucco, Dennis Reardon, and Pat Toomay.

About the Author

David Rabe has been hailed as one of America's greatest living playwrights. He is the author of many widely performed plays, including *The Basic Training of Pavlo Hummel, Sticks and Bones, In the Boom Boom Room, Streamers, Hurlyburly,* and *The Dog Problem.* Four of his plays have been nominated for the Tony Award, including one win for best play. He is the recipient of an Obie Award, the American Academy of Arts and Letters Award, the Drama Desk Award, and the New York Drama Critics Circle Award, among others.

Rabe is the critically acclaimed author of the novels *Dinosaurs on the Roof* and *Recital of the Dog,* and a collection of short stories, *A Primitive Heart.* Born in Dubuque, Iowa, Rabe lives with his family in northwest Connecticut.

Printed in the United States
By Bookmasters